New York City Docs

Hot-shot surgeons,
taking the world by storm…
by day and by night!

In the heart of New York City, four friends
sharing an apartment in Brooklyn are on
their way to becoming the best there is at the
prestigious West Manhattan Saints Hospital—
and these driven docs will
let *nothing* stand in their way!

Meet Tessa, Kimberlyn, Holly and Sam
as they strive to save lives and become
top-notch surgeons in the Big Apple.
Trained by world-class experts,
these young docs are the future—and they're
taking the medical world by storm.

But with all their time dedicated to patients,
late nights and long shifts, the last thing they
expect is to meet the loves of their lives!

For fast-paced drama and sizzling romance,
check out the *New York City Docs* quartet:

Hot Doc from Her Past
Tina Beckett

Surgeons, Rivals…Lovers
Amalie Berlin

Falling at the Surgeon's Feet
Lucy Ryder

One Night in New York
Amy Ruttan

Available from February 2016!

Dear Reader,

Thank you for picking up a copy of *One Night in New York*.

I had a lot of fun writing this book, and I had a great time plotting out this series with my fellow quad authors Tina Beckett, Amalie Berlin and Lucy Ryder. Lots of giggling was to be had.

In its past, New York City was the city where immigrants found a chance to start again. It's a city that's alive and vibrant. It's the kind of city my heroine needs. It's a place where she can find herself again after her heartbreaking divorce.

My hero is no stranger to New York, but he too finds out who he really is and who he is as a doctor, just about to start on the path he's always dreamed of and step out of the shadows as a brilliant paediatric surgeon. New York is the city of dreams, after all.

To paraphrase that great song 'New York, New York' and Ol' Blue Eyes: If my characters can make it here, they can make it anywhere.

I love hearing from readers, so please drop by my website, www.amyruttan.com, or give me a shout on Twitter @ruttanamy.

With warmest wishes

Amy Ruttan

ONE NIGHT
IN NEW YORK

BY
AMY RUTTAN

First published in Great Britain 2015
By Mills & Boon, an imprint of HarperCollins*Publishers*
1 London Bridge Street, London, SE1 9GF

Large Print edition 2016

© 2015 Amy Ruttan

ISBN: 978-0-263-26081-6

Born and raised on the outskirts of Toronto, Ontario, **Amy Ruttan** fled the big city to settle down with the country boy of her dreams. When she's not furiously typing away at her computer she's mom to three wonderful children, who have given her another job as a taxi driver. A voracious reader, she was given her first romance novel by her grandmother, who shared her penchant for a hot romance. From that moment Amy was hooked by the magical worlds, handsome heroes and sigh-worthy romances contained in the pages, and she knew what she wanted to be when she grew up. Life got in the way, but after the birth of her second child she decided to pursue her dream of becoming a romance author.

Amy loves to hear from readers. It makes her day, in fact. You can find out more about Amy at her website: amyruttan.com.

Books by Amy Ruttan

Mills & Boon Medical Romance

Safe in His Hands
Melting the Ice Queen's Heart
Pregnant with the Soldier's Son
Dare She Date Again?
It Happened in Vegas
Taming Her Navy Doc

Visit the Author Profile page at millsandboon.co.uk for more titles.

This book is dedicated to my fellow quartet authors: Tina Beckett, Amalie Berlin and Lucy Ryder. Thank you, ladies, for such an awesome experience. I had so much fun creating an exciting world with you and bringing West Manhattan Saints to life.

Praise for
Amy Ruttan

'I highly recommend this for all fans of romance reads with amazing, absolutely breathtaking scenes, to-die-for dialogue, and everything else that is needed to make this a beyond awesome and WOW read!'

—Goodreads on
Melting the Ice Queen's Heart

'A sensational romance, filled with astounding medical drama. Author Amy Ruttan makes us visualise the story with her flawless storytelling. The emotional and sensory details are exquisitely done and the sensuality in the love scene just sizzles. Highly recommended for all lovers of medical romance.'

—Contemporary Romance Reviews on
Safe in His Heart

CHAPTER ONE

Manhattan, winter

THE BAR WASN'T particularly packed tonight, but that wasn't overly strange as it was the middle of the week. Still, as Sam Napier peered around the glitzy nightclub on the Upper West Side, far from his local watering hole in Brooklyn, there were a few glitterati mingling, drinks in their hands, trying to escape the wintry blast of cold air outside. It was a good night to people-watch and he had nothing else to do.

He leaned back against the bar, sipping his Scotch and people-watching. This was a place where he could just melt into the woodwork, if there was any wood in the chrome and glass bar, and no one knew who he was. It was nice.

The local watering hole in Brooklyn was great,

but there would be a ninety-nine point nine percent chance that he would run into someone from work and/or one of his roommates and tonight he didn't want that. He didn't need to talk about how there was a new attending who could possibly mess with his future at West Manhattan Saints Hospital.

Besides, Enzo, his closest friend, had paired up with Sam's roommate Kimberlyn and those two had recently moved to Tennessee. His other roommate, Tessa, had moved out and there was no way he could handle the *girl* talk with Holly his only current roommate, though some more were moving in. Just the thought of her chattering made him shudder.

There was no one to commiserate with. No close friends and those he was close to wouldn't expect him to open up anyway. He kept most things to himself, but tonight he really needed to drown his sorrows. No one would understand that one of the department heads who had a say in his appointment as a pediatric fellow had retired and a new replacement surgeon had been appointed. And apparently the surgeon replacing Dr. Powers, the former Head of Obstetrics and Maternal-Fetal Medicine, was one of the top surgeons in the field and a slave-driver.

But Sam didn't see the need for maternal-fetal medicine at West Manhattan Saints. Dr. Amelia Chang, Head of Pediatrics, could handle most issues in utero with the OB/GYN, and even then they could send the patient on to a larger hospital if necessary.

In all Sam's years at West Manhattan Saints he'd barely seen Dr. Powers in surgery. So why did she need a replacement for such a small department? The obstetrics department at West Manhattan Saints was not large. The hospital was known for trauma, with Dr. Ootaka at the helm, and Pediatrics.

This new attending was a waste of money as far as Sam was concerned. But not surprising, given who the chief of surgery was. This new attending was probably BFFs with Professor Gareth Langley.

Great. Just what he needed: another egotistical, maniacal surgeon like the chief of surgery at West Manhattan Saints or, worse, like his mother…

At least he'd learned one thing from her numerous failed relationships and dalliances: successful surgeons couldn't have a family.

"You need to find someone, Sam. You're lonely." Kimberlyn's plea popped into his mind. *"I know some nice girls,"* she had said repeatedly.

Sam had always rebuffed her. The last thing he wanted was a relationship. He didn't have time for one. Still, he kind of wished sometimes he had someone, even if just for a moment.

Sam was knocked out of his reverie and his drink was splashed down the front of his sweater when he was whacked by an icy wet scarf.

"Holy crackers! It's cold out there," a big puffy yeti said, sitting down on the bar stool next to him as it began to pull off its layers.

"Bloody hell…"

"Oh, my God. I'm so sorry." As the last layer came off a beautiful redheaded vixen reached for a napkin and began to dab at his sweater in a futile attempt to soak up the expensive Scotch that had seeped into the fibers. "I can't believe I did that. I didn't see you there."

"Obviously not." Sam wiped away the chunk of snow that was melting in his eye. "Then again, I don't how much you could see with that many layers on. It's not that cold outside, lass."

Her brown eyes widened. "You're Scottish."

"Half," he mumbled, snatching the napkin from her hand and trying to fix the damage to his sweater himself. When he got agitated his accent came out thicker. His mother was American, but since his father had mostly raised him in the Highlands he had more Scot in him than Yankee, though he had been born in Manhattan at the hospital he was currently completing his residency in.

"I hope it's not designer," she said with concern.

"What's not?" Sam asked confused.

"The sweater."

He chuckled. "Hardly. No, it's not designer. I just like it, that's all."

And he did. His gran had knitted it for him. It was a blue-gray V-neck sweater, which had seen better days, but it gave him a sense of home.

She smiled, a lovely warm one that made his heart skip a beat. There was something about red-haired women that made him melt just a bit. Maybe it was something about gingers sticking together, even though his hair was more auburn and hers was a bit more mahogany than the classic ginger.

Bloody hell. Why am I analyzing hair color? How many drinks have I had?

Then he remembered the Scotch currently soaked into his sweater had been his first and he'd only had a taste of it.

"I'm really sorry. Can I replace the drink I spilled?" she asked.

"That you can do."

"I have to say I'm disappointed."

"How so?" he asked.

"I thought you were going to answer me with 'Aye.'"

Sam laughed. "No, I only save that for when I'm really tetchy. My name is Sam, by the way."

"Mindy." She held out her hand and he took it in his, brushing a quick kiss across her knuckles, which made her gasp.

He heard it and it pleased him to know he'd gotten that response out of her. Something his dear old dad had taught him.

"A pleasure to meet you, Mindy." Sam was still holding her hand as she stared up at him for a moment, her eyes wide, her pink lips open, but only for a moment then pink tinged her cheeks and she took back her hand.

"It's a pleasure to meet you." She cleared her throat and turned to the barkeeper. "One Merlot and a…?"

"Scotch."

The barkeep nodded and moved away. Sam took the bar stool next to her. "So, I take it you're not from around these parts."

"What makes you say that?" she asked.

"You were bundled up enough to make a trek to the South Pole."

Mindy chuckled. "I'm really not used to the cold."

"I gathered that."

The barkeeper returned with their drinks and Mindy slid him some money. He could just say thanks for the drink and move on, really he should, but she was just the kind of distraction from his own problems that he was looking for. It had been some time since he'd indulged, he'd been so focused on his residency. He never entered into one-night situations, because he refused to follow in the same footsteps as his mother, but maybe tonight if Mindy was interested he could relent, just a bit.

"Where are you from?" Sam asked.

"California. Born and raised. And where are you from?"

"Here," Sam replied, winking at her.

"Oh, come on. I told you mine, now tell me yours."

"Well, I was born in Manhattan, but I was raised in the Highlands by my father."

"How interesting." She took a sip of her wine. "Was he a laird?"

It was meant as a tease. He knew it. It always was.

"Aye, he is."

Mindy choked on her wine. "You're not serious?"

"I am. Very. Did you not hear my 'Aye'?"

"I thought that was only saved for when you were tetchy?"

"Or when I'm *very* serious." He winked at her.

"He's a laird?"

"It's not as romantic as you're thinking it is. It just means he owns a large bit of land in the Highlands. He doesn't serve out justice to his lowly tenants. He's not nobility."

"So what does that make you?"

"Make me?"

"Or are there other heirs apparent?" She winked as she took a sip of her Merlot.

Sam laughed. "I'm the eldest, but really it

doesn't make me anything other than what you see here."

Mindy cocked her head to one side. "And here I thought I was talking to royalty."

Sam chuckled. "Hardly. So what brought you from the warm confines of California to the harsh and bitter environment of Manhattan?"

"You're mocking me, aren't you?"

"Just a wee bit."

Mindy sighed and tucked a long strand of mahogany hair behind her ear. "A new job and a new...start."

"I can tell from your tone that you wanted to get as far away from California as possible."

"How can you tell that from my tone?"

"It was tight, like you were in pain."

What are you doing?

As Mindy glanced over at the devilishly handsome man, warmth spread through her, a zing of something she hadn't felt in quite some time.

Maybe it's the wine?

No, not the wine. Even when she'd still been

with Dean, the last few years of their marriage had been detached and they had just been going through the motions. Of course, she'd thought it was their careers that had kept them apart, she'd never suspected someone else and she had certainly never expected that someone else to be her best friend and colleague. Dean and Owen's betrayal cut her to the quick. She'd trusted Dean. He had been her husband and he betrayed her.

Trust was something she never gave freely. She'd been burned so many times by so-called friends. She'd thought she'd been able to trust her husband. The one person who'd held her heart. So when he'd done the unthinkable she'd had a hard time believing in any one else, in trusting another person. Intimacy was a huge leap of faith, letting someone see that vulnerable side to you.

So, yeah, it had been a long time since she'd even contemplated thinking about a man in a sexual way. It had been a while since a tingle of excitement at the possibility of something more had revved her motor, but when his lips brushed against her knuckles suddenly the cold winter temperatures had no longer bothered her.

Sam's blue eyes were twinkling mischievously. He was a bad boy. There was no mistaking it, but the way he leaned against the bar, the emotional walls he had in place, the devilry in those blue, blue eyes. Sam was the kind of man her mother had always warned her to steer clear of. Yet it had been the *nice* man, the respectable one, whom her mother had approved of, who had betrayed her trust.

Besides, she was just flirting with this handsome heir of a Scottish laird in an upscale Manhattan bar. It didn't have to go any further than this.

Why not?

It might be nice to cut loose and celebrate a new life, at a new hospital. Tonight she didn't have to be a world-renowned maternal-fetal surgeon. Tonight she just had to be Mindy. She'd never see this guy again. He wouldn't use her or hurt her.

She could just be Mindy. Lonely and scared out of her mind Mindy, but still...

What was he saying? Oh, yes, he thought she sounded in pain. Great.

She giggled nervously.

Maybe he sensed she needed a change of topic because he asked, "So, what makes me so funny, then? Is it the accent that amuses you so much? Or is it my boyish charm?" He waggled his eyebrows suggestively, making her melt just a bit.

"Boyish charm for sure." She smiled at him, which was easy to do. She couldn't recall ever smiling and flirting with Dean, but, then, she had always been a wallflower. Shy and meek. This was new, it felt good. She picked up her drink and took a sip, wincing at the burn of alcohol. Honestly, she didn't know why she'd ordered wine, she wasn't much of a drinker.

"Something wrong with your wine?" Sam asked.

"No, nothing. It's fine. I don't usually go to bars."

"Then can I ask why you wanted to brave the

harsh, bitter environment of winter to come to a bar and suffer through what looks to be a very painful glass of wine."

Mindy shrugged. "As I said, I'm new here. I wanted to meet people."

Sam leaned over. "*Well*, you've met me."

"You're laying it on very thick now."

"It amuses me to do so." He cleared his throat and then swigged down the last of his Scotch. "There, that's better. My mellow American accent is back. What do you think?"

"I prefer the Scottish one." Then she giggled.

It was pathetic that she was giggling. It had been a while since she'd dated or flirted, but when you spent your whole career operating on such delicate humans as fetuses you didn't really have much of a life. Not when their tiny little lives were in your hands. Not when their mothers' lives were in your hands. She spent a lot of time in research, in ORs, sitting by patients' bedsides.

Too many happy families depended on her and

being one of the top surgeons in her field meant she was in high demand.

There was no time for socializing or anything else. She'd met Dean when they had both been interns, learning under the same surgeon. They'd both been maternal-fetal specialists. They'd both been on the same trajectory.

Or so she'd thought.

"Dean, don't you want to have kids? I'm ready. I think we're ready."

"We're not ready, Mindy. You just think you're ready. You work around kids and babies all day long. We have to focus on our careers now. Once we're both really settled and in the top of our chosen fields, then we'll settle down. We'll have a couple of kids."

And then that had never happened and now it wouldn't happen because, number one, she was no longer Dean's wife, number two, he was still in California, and, number three, Dean was gay.

There had been a lot of sniggers in the private practice she'd worked at in Los Angeles with Dean about how she'd found out he'd been cheating on her. Mindy had known Owen was gay, he had been her best friend. She didn't care that Dean was gay, it was the fact that he'd gone behind her back and cheated on her with Owen and that the two of them had been carrying on for over a year and hadn't told her. She'd shared her insecurities with Owen about her marriage. She'd trusted him too and he'd used those secret hurts and concerns against her.

That's what had hurt the most. Dean knew everything she'd told Owen.

"You look angry all of a sudden. Are you okay?" Sam asked, breaking her out of her thoughts.

"I'm fine." Well, she wasn't. Not really. She was still letting Dean and Owen get to her. Even though it had been a year since her divorce had been finalized.

Dean and Owen had moved on and were in the process of adopting a child.

A child. Mindy had wanted a child for five years, but Dean had never been ready and Owen had told her not to push Dean on the matter.

"I'm fine," she said again, and swigged back the last of her Merlot. "Just. Fine."

So many years of her life wasted. Too many.

"I don't think you are." Sam got up. "Do you want me to walk you home?"

"You can do more than walk me home." She wasn't sure if it was the wine or what, but she grabbed the collar of Sam's sweater, or where there would've been a collar if he wasn't wearing a V-neck, and pulled him close to her, planting a kiss on his lips because she had to see for herself if those lips against hers would be just as thrilling as when they'd brushed against her knuckles.

And God help her. They were.

Stop. Stop. Stop.

Only she couldn't. His arms went around her, his strong hands on her back as their bodies pressed together. The kiss deepened, so even if she wanted to turn back now she couldn't. It had been so long since she'd had this kind of human contact.

So long that she'd forgotten what it was like

and maybe even forgotten that she craved it, to have a man be aroused by *her* and not by her best friend.

Just her.

Sam broke off the kiss. "If you continue to do that I don't think I'll be able to stop."

"What if I don't want you to stop?"

Sam's blue eyes twinkled. "Well, then, that's a whole different story."

"My apartment is next door."

He grinned. "Oh, aye?"

"Yeah." Mindy grabbed her copious layers and took his hand, leading him out of the bar. She was going to be impulsive. *Even if it was just this once in her life.* She was going to live a little and she was going to do it with this dishy Scottish laird heir, or whoever he claimed to be.

She just needed this.

She badly needed to wipe the slate clean.

"Hold on. I just need to get my jacket. I may be more used to the winters than you, but I don't want to freeze out there."

"Sorry, I wasn't thinking."

He grinned and winked at her. "It's okay. For a moment I wasn't thinking either. I was just thinking about kissing you again." Then he leaned in, brushing his knuckles down the side of her face, which made her knees go weak, just before he kissed her. A light kiss that made her whole body tingle with anticipation.

Mindy watched the dishy Scot go to the coat check and slip on his jacket.

She couldn't believe that she was actually doing this, that she was taking a strange man home to her apartment to have sex with. A younger man to boot.

In all her thirty-seven years she'd never done anything like this. She'd never lived dangerously. She was always too afraid to take the chance, to take the risk. Except when it came to surgery. When she was in the OR it gave her a whole different kind of rush. When she was in the OR and a mother and her baby's lives were in jeopardy she went with her gut instinct. It was the same instinct she was using now.

Mindy was trying to listen to her gut more

often, especially about non-medical situations. She'd been terrified about leaving California, which was safe and what she knew, but she'd listened to her gut and made the decision to travel across country.

So when she'd seen Sam and spoken with him, her gut had told her to take a chance, to live a little. She hadn't been with anyone since Dean and even then that had been some time ago.

It was time to start afresh.

She could do this and, more importantly, she wanted to do this.

He joined her. "Lead the way."

Mindy's cheeks flushed with heat and she knew she was blushing, but she didn't care as she took his hand. They walked across the street to her condo. The doorman let her in and didn't even bat an eyelash over the fact that she had gone to the bar alone less than an hour ago and was returning with a man.

They got into the elevator and she hit the button to her floor.

"Penthouse?" he remarked.

"It's the best."

The elevator stopped and they walked down the hall to her apartment. She was shaking. She was very nervous about what was going to happen, but she wanted it to happen.

"Here it is," she said, hoping that her voice didn't wobble too much.

Get a grip on yourself, Mindy! You're not some inexperienced virgin. You've done this before.

"Are you nervous, Mindy?" he asked.

"A bit."

"Look, we don't have to do this. I won't be mad."

He was being a gentleman. He was giving her a way out, but she didn't want a way out. She wanted this. She needed this night. Tomorrow she was going to start her new job and she wouldn't have time for moments like this.

As of tomorrow she planned to focus solely on building her career and her patient list at West Manhattan Saints. There would be no time for dating, gorgeous men or trysts. It was now or never.

"No, I want this. It's just that I've…I've never done this before."

He smiled at her tenderly, stroking her face. "I have a confession."

"Oh, yes?"

"I haven't done this for a very long time, and if you want to stop at any moment, I'll stop. I won't force you, I won't pressure you."

Mindy smiled and then kissed him, just like she had in the bar. His arms came around her, their bodies pressed together.

"I want this." She unlocked the door to her apartment and pulled him inside.

There was no turning back now for her.

CHAPTER TWO

SAM HURRIED DOWN the hall of West Manhattan Saints at a quick pace, but considering he was late it was a pace that wasn't quick enough for his liking. He'd been reluctant to leave that temptress's bed this morning, but he had and before she'd woken up.

Which was good. He didn't want to deal with any aftermath. At least her apartment was close to the hospital, but he was still late. He was never late and people would notice. It wasn't good.

Not when today was the day the new head of maternal-fetal medicine was being introduced to the peds floor. He'd barely made it to the hospital in time for a shower and a fresh set of scrubs. His sweater, currently hanging in his locker, still smelled strongly of Scotch. He straightened the

collar of his white lab coat and slung his stethoscope around his neck without missing a beat.

"Holly said you didn't make it home last night,"
Rebecca, their new roommate, teased as she fell
into step beside him.

"Since when did you become my keeper?"

"You're tetchy this morning. What happened
last night?"

"Nothing. Look, shouldn't you be on the
trauma floor?" Sam asked, trying to get rid of
Rebecca before she pried too much deeper. His
roommate didn't need to know that he'd had a
one-night stand. He didn't know her well enough
yet and she seemed to report everything back
to Holly, Tessa or Kimberlyn. And those three
were always purporting to know nice girls to set
him up with. The three of them were in cahoots.

Sam figured it had something to do with the
fact that he had been the only male in the brownstone for some time. Not to mention that they
were all loved up themselves and seemed determined to push soulmatedom on everyone else.

"Heading there now. Just wanted to wish you good luck with the new head. I hear she's tough."

Sam grunted his thanks as Rebecca headed down another hallway that led back to Trauma and he kept on his course to Peds. Before he pushed open the rainbow-colored double doors that led into the pediatric department, he straightened his hair in the reflection of the mirror.

There was already a crowd gathering in the main thoroughfare of the department, right in front of the main charge desk. Sam could see Dr. Amelia Chang talking calmly to the group of surgeons who were all vying for the two coveted fellowship positions in Peds.

As he moved into the group he caught Dr. Chang's gaze and could see she was quite aware that he was late. Her quiet disapproval and disappointment was hard to miss.

Mother would not be impressed.

At least Dr. Chang wouldn't humiliate him and call him out on the carpet for being late. His mother's way of teaching her residents was shaming them so they didn't do it again. Dr.

Chang would probably put him on scut duty. Labs and charting he could deal with.

"Now that we're all here, we can finally get down to business. As you are all aware, this pediatric fellowship is one of the top five on the eastern seaboard, and we can only open this fellowship to two worthy residents. Because of that, the hospital has always felt that those two positions should not be decided solely by the pediatric head. That's why the head of Neonatology, Dr. Hall, taking over from Dr. Powers, the head of Obstetrics, Dr. Finn, and also the new head of Maternal-Fetal Medicine will *all* have a say in who gets those two spots." Dr. Chang leaned against the charge desk, her eyes scanning the crowd, silently assessing them in that unnerving way she had before continuing.

"I know some of you have questioned the need for Maternal-Fetal Medicine to have an impact on your career as a pediatric fellow at West Manhattan Saints. We don't see a lot of births that require a need for that, but that is changing. West Manhattan Saints hopes to become an innovative leader in maternal-fetal medicine and high-risk pregnancies. We will be expanding our birthing center to accommodate high-risk pregnancies."

Sam was stunned, but pleased that this new head wasn't a waste of resources and he could see the potential of Labor and Delivery, Neonatology and Pediatrics hand in hand to become one of the best hospitals on the eastern seaboard. Still, how many high-risk pregnancies could they possibly see?

"As you know, Dr. Powers retired, and after many years of excellent service we wish her the best. Thankfully, Professor Langley was able to find a replacement for the maternal-fetal role, which means the selection for fellowship won't be delayed any longer. Dr. Walker is one of the top maternal-fetal surgeons from California."

A knot of dread formed in Sam's stomach and he quickly scanned the room and then saw Dr. Walker approaching the group. He couldn't believe what he was seeing.

Mindy.

The vixen from last night, the bumbling yeti who had spilled his Scotch and then seduced him, was walking with Dr. Finn. She looked so different from last night. All that glorious, silken mahogany hair was tied back and she wore black square glasses with only light lip gloss. Her look was demure, professional, but as Sam let his gaze rove over her, her appearance didn't fool him. He knew what was lurking under the surface and just the thought of her in his arms and under him caused his blood to boil.

This was *not* good. Not the sex, that had been beyond good, but the fact that it had been with one of his new bosses was *not good*. If he had known that, he would've walked away from her. He refused to follow the same path as his mother. She'd used sex to get what she wanted when she'd been a young surgeon and he'd seen how that had broken his father's heart.

He wanted to get the fellowship on his own merits, because he had talent. He wanted to prove to his mother that he had what it took to be the very best, to get where he was without sleeping his way there. He'd show her.

Mindy's appearance was bad.

Very bad.

He tried to move to the back of the crowd, but it was too late. She looked out over the crowd, and that bright smile faded, wavering slightly as their gazes locked.

"Without further ado I would like to introduce the new head of Maternal-Fetal Medicine, Dr. Mindy Walker."

Mindy blushed slightly and broke the visual connection as she came up beside Dr. Chang, shaking her hand as everyone applauded her politely.

Sam tried to swallow the lump in his throat as he pretended that he didn't know her. Even though no one else had seemed to notice the interplay between the two of them, he felt singled out.

Why did it have to be her? Why did his only one-night stand in the last three years have to be someone who was responsible for the fate of his career?

Bloody fates.

He slid his attention back to Mindy, who was now addressing the crowd.

"I want to thank everyone here. I'm a perfectionist when it comes to my specialty. I don't tolerate a lot of things when it comes to my surgical practice. Fragile lives are in our hands. There is no time for mistakes and because I'm new to this hospital and have yet to get to know all of you, I'll be requesting each one of you to work on my rotation for at least a week or more before I make any decisions about who will be getting a fellowship. My department is not large by any means yet. I'm also one of the top IVF and fertility doctors in the country. I'm a board certified OB/GYN. Pregnancy and the safe of arrival of babies and their mothers are my passion. One I take seriously." She paused, her gaze penetrating him, and it was then Sam knew he was in trouble. Deep trouble.

"I look forward to working with all of you."

She turned and began to chat with Dr. Chang and the other heads.

Everyone clapped politely as the crowd dispersed to start their rounds. What else could they do? The committee had the control over the fellowship. He just had to make sure he kept his nose down and worked hard.

And keep his distance.

Sam tried to slip away with the crowd.

"Dr. Napier, could you come here a moment, please?" Dr. Chang called out.

So much for slinking off and going unnoticed today.

He turned around and walked over to Dr. Chang and Dr. Walker. Mindy's face was expressionless as he approached them.

"Yes, Dr. Chang?" He said his words carefully, because he didn't want his Scottish accent to bubble up. He'd told Mindy that it surfaced when his emotions weren't in check.

"You were late this morning. Are you okay?" Dr. Chang asked.

"I..." He tried not to make eye contact with

Mindy, who had a pink tinge to her cheeks. "I overslept, that's all. It won't happen again."

Dr. Chang nodded, assessing him. He hated disappointing her. She embodied everything great in pediatric surgery and he wanted one of the fellowship spots. It's why he had been willing to come to West Manhattan Saints and work in a hospital that had ties to his mother and ties to Professor Langley, who was the first man his mother had had an affair with.

Sam detested Langley, but having a chance to work and learn beside Dr. Amelia Chang? He could put aside all his animosity for that.

"See that it doesn't," Dr. Chang said.

"I'll make sure of it, Dr. Chang."

"Dr. Walker has requested you join her service for the first rotation."

Sam cringed inwardly. "Of course."

"It's a great honor to learn from her. The skills you'll learn from her will be invaluable." Dr. Chang didn't say any more as she walked away, presumably to start her rounds. The only people around the charge station now were him and Mindy.

No. Not Mindy. Dr. Walker.

Well, whoever she was. She looked none too pleased to see him.

"Dr. Napier?" Her eyes were positively flinty, her arms crossed and her lips pursed together in a thin line. Sam wasn't exactly sure how she got the words out.

"Dr. Walker," he acknowledged. He wanted to ask her why she hadn't told him what her job was, but, then, the conversation last night had never really stretched to that.

"Well, I hope you have a good understanding of high-risk pregnancies and have clocked some hours in OB/GYN and genetics. My caseload here is heavy. I have mothers coming in from a lot of different hospitals, some as far west as California, to seek my professional help. I don't want an inept surgeon bumbling around in my OR."

She was clearly angry.

"I can assure you I'm one of the top residents in this program, Dr. Walker."

Mindy snorted. "That remains to be seen."

"What do you mean by that?" Sam asked.

"You know what I mean," she snapped under her breath. "Don't think sleeping with me gains you any extra footing here, Dr. Napier. In fact, it's detrimental to your position in this program. I don't play favorites."

Sam vibrated with anger and without thinking he grabbed Mindy by her arm and dragged her to the nearest empty exam room, not caring who saw them. Which was saying a whole lot. He hated drawing attention to himself, but suggesting he'd slept with her to get ahead? That was taking it too far.

He was here to work hard for himself. He needed to nip this in the bud. He didn't want any rumors flying around.

And he wasn't going to allow a rumor to destroy his career, his reputation.

He pushed her into the exam room, flicked on

the light, shut the door and stood in front of it, stopping her only means of escape.

"Do you think I slept with you to *gain footing*? If that's what you think, you had better change your opinion right now." His brogue was coming out very thickly, but he couldn't control it.

He was angry.

Very angry.

Mindy was shaking with a mixture of anger and betrayal.

Dammit.

Of course the one time she had a one-night stand it had to be with a surgical resident and one she was going to have direct involvement with. The day before she'd slept with Sam, she'd been going over the residents' files, reading over notes from other attendings, reports from other doctors and patients.

Dr. Samuel Napier was well respected, admired and most if not all of the surgeons who worked with him commented on his bedside manner with pediatric patients and his skill in the operating room. Though he dealt more with older children than babies.

She'd earmarked him as one to watch, but hadn't intended to choose him as her first resident. Her process was to weed out the weaker members of the herd. Mindy had had another resident in mind, but when she'd walked into that meeting and learned that her hot, brooding one-night stand was none other than Dr. Samuel Napier she had been absolutely furious.

No wonder he got good reports.

He probably slept with all his attendings. Not a hard thing to do when most of the surgeons in Pediatrics at this hospital were female. He'd used her. She knew she shouldn't have let her guard down, because she couldn't trust anyone.

And now he'd frog-marched her into this exam room to give her a talking-to? And she was his superior? No, this wasn't happening. Mindy refused to be pushed around again.

"I'm not changing my opinion of you just because you say that I should. Why should I trust you? You didn't even tell me you worked at the hospital, that you were a surgical resident."

Sam's eyes narrowed, those delectable lips which she could still feel imprinted against her body, were pursed together.

"You *didn't* tell me *you* were a surgeon either."

"I did too."

A diabolical grin spread across Sam's face. "No, you didn't."

Mindy opened her mouth to argue further and realized through those hazy, jangled memories of their meeting in the bar that all she'd told him had been her first name and that she'd moved to New York to start a new job, but not what that job was.

"You know that I'm right." His grin turned smug and he leaned against the door.

"You could've still looked up my CV online once you learned about the new head of Maternal-Fetal Medicine and our meeting was just an opportune moment."

The grin disappeared. "I did not sleep with you for personal gain. I'm extremely good at my job, so if you need to test me, so be it. I will take whatever challenge you have for me, and gladly. Though it's a waste of time."

Mindy snorted. "You think that maternal-fetal medicine and working on my service is a waste of time?"

"I do. My plan is to work with Dr. Chang and become a pediatric surgeon. Infants go to the NICU or the neonatologist. You're just a glorified obstetrician."

Mindy shook her head. "You're a bit arrogant, aren't you?"

"You have to be in this line of work. You have to be tough for the patients, for the parents and you have to be that tough to swim in this shark tank."

"You think surgery is a shark tank?"

"I do. Don't you?"

Mindy couldn't argue with him on that. It was. She'd learned the hard way that you couldn't trust other surgeons, especially not when you had ten or more residents competing for OR time, competing for attendings' attention and competing for only a couple of spots in a small fellowship pool.

When she'd entered surgery she hadn't been a shark. Dean and Owen had been sharks, but she hadn't. All she'd had had been raw talent. It used to infuriate Dean when she was chosen over him when they'd been residents. That should've been a clue.

Well, now she was one and she wasn't going to let an arrogant resident think that she wasn't. She needed to be tough. When she'd taken this job and uprooted her life to start fresh in New York City, she'd known she was going to have to be a shark from the get-go.

"Well, I guess I'll be wasting your time, but know this, some of those pediatric patients' problems start in utero. You think my specialty is a waste of time? Let me tell you something. The more my specialty advances, the more genetics advances and the more likely your job as a pediatric surgeon will become obsolete. Operating and taking care of those issues while the baby is still in utero will save them countless surgeries later in life. Dr. Chang is an excellent pediatric surgeon, but she doesn't have the skill to operate in utero. If people like me have our way, all pediatric problems will be taken care of while still in the protective walls of the womb and there will be less children on the pediatric floor." She moved closer to him. "Soon pediatric surgeons will be like the dinosaurs. Extinct."

Sam didn't say anything. In fact, for a moment he looked at bit shocked.

"So you think my specialty, my service is a waste of time? Well, I won't hold you to your rotation on my service, but I can tell you, Dr. Napier, that I won't be basing my vote on a resident who isn't willing to graciously learn all the specialties that are involved with taking care of children."

Mindy tried to move past him, still shaking.

"Wait." Sam grabbed her arm to stop her.

He was so close. Only a couple of hours ago he'd been in her bed. When she'd woken up and he'd been gone, it had stung, but she had been almost euphoric and definitely relaxed when she'd got into work. Until she'd seen him standing with the residents.

It had been like a slap to the face.

Just reaffirming to her that she couldn't trust men. They were all users.

"I'm sorry, Dr. Walker."

Mindy was stunned. "Thank you, Dr. Napier."

"I'll gladly work on your service and I'll prove to you my merit as a surgeon, but please know that I didn't sleep with you because you were my attending. Had I known, I would've kept as far away from you as possible. Nothing will taint my career at this hospital, or my chance to become a fellow in Dr. Chang's program. Nothing."

As Mindy looked up at Sam she wanted to believe him, but couldn't. "Okay. I'll give you a fair chance, Dr. Napier, but one toe out of line..."

"The implication is clear." He let go of her arm

and stepped away from the door. "I look forward to learning from you, Dr. Walker."

Mindy nodded. She was pleased that she'd gotten through to him, but she could see the barriers, ones that had come down just a teeny bit last night, were building again. Walls that were meant to keep people out, from knowing the true Sam.

She didn't know the true version of him. Maybe if circumstances had been different, if something more could've stemmed from their night of passion, she might know the real Sam who remained locked behind those protective walls.

There could've been something more there.

Whatever he was protecting, it ran deep and Mindy would never know.

It was for the best.

She was his boss; he was a resident. That's all it could ever be, but she couldn't help but feel an inkling of regret.

"I'll see you at rounds in thirty minutes." Mindy didn't look at him, but he didn't stop her from leaving this time, which was good, because she had to distance herself from him emotionally.

Dr. Samuel Napier was off-limits, even if she didn't want him to be.

CHAPTER THREE

SAM STOOD BACK because the ER was absolutely packed full of casualties from a multi-car pile-up. Usually, he'd be right into the fray, helping, but Mindy didn't want him to so much as touch a patient.

There were more than enough trauma residents and general surgeon residents to lend a helping hand.

Mindy wanted him watching as she assessed an injured pregnant mother. One who was only twenty-six weeks. Mindy and neonatologist Dr. Hall were assessing the mother in a trauma pod and Sam was watching them.

Which kind of annoyed him. Greatly. He wanted to be in the throng, helping the wounded. This was going against the grain for him.

As he scanned the medical staff out on the

floor he could see at least two residents he knew doing what they did best. Practicing medicine.

Rebecca looked up from where he was working and shot him a look of *What gives?* And all Sam could do was shrug. He had his orders. He was to observe. Very similar to his mother's methods.

Don't think about her now.

"Get out of the way!" Dr. Chang's voice was shrill above the din and he watched as she ran beside a gurney, a little body wrapped up and bagged, as they pushed through the crowds toward the surgical floor.

Sam's gut instinct was to run after Dr. Chang and that child. Every fiber of his being screamed at him to go.

"Dr. Napier?"

Sam cursed under his breath as he turned around.

"Distracted?" Mindy asked, slinging her stethoscope around her neck.

"No."

Her eyes narrowed. "Well, Ms. Bayberry is

your responsibility. Get her up to Ultrasound and monitor her contractions. She's pregnant with twins and was involved in the collision. We're looking for signs of pre-term labor. Also contact her current practitioner. I'd like her updated files about her pregnancy."

"Isn't that best left to an intern?" he asked, annoyed that he wasn't with Dr. Chang.

Mindy crossed her arms. "I asked you to do it, Dr. Napier. Do you have a problem with that?"

"No. Of course not." Sam moved passed Mindy toward Ms. Bayberry's bed. Dr. Hall ignored him as she conferred with Mindy about the treatment should poor Ms. Bayberry go into labor.

"Will my babies be okay?" Ms. Bayberry asked nervously, her eyes wide with fear. This was the part of the job he hated the most, when he couldn't answer the patient's questions.

"Will this treatment help my son?"

"Will this cure him?"

It tugged at his heartstrings. It ate him up inside and he didn't know where the parents found strength. He'd talked to his father about that once, after watching children struggle with life-threatening conditions. It scared him, bringing a child into the world, and for one moment, when he had first been starting his residency and focusing on pediatrics, he'd thought about leaving and following in his mother's footsteps.

"I don't know how you do it. How do you find the strength when your child is sick?"

"You just do. What else can you do? You give them everything. That's what being a parent is," his father had said. *"I would do anything for you and your brothers. I don't care what happens to me. Only my children matter."*

And as Ms. Bayberry looked up at him, fear in her eyes, it affected him. Only he couldn't let her see it. For her, he had to be strong so that she could be strong for her babies, but he couldn't promise her anything.

That was something he learned from his mother.

Never promise a patient something you couldn't deliver with one hundred percent certainty. Even though Ms. Bayberry was in the best hands with Mindy, of that he was sure, he didn't know the future so he could only offer her what he could to ease her mind.

"You're in the best hands, Ms. Bayberry. Let's get you upstairs for some scans." And he smiled at her and she relaxed. Though she was still terrified, he could see a bit of that fear dissipating and the goal was to keep her calm.

He was taking some vitals and making sure the machines monitoring her contractions were ready to transport when he glanced up.

Mindy was watching him. She wasn't listening to Dr. Hall her gaze was focused on him. He wasn't sure if it was with admiration or surprise, but whatever it was it made his heart beat just a bit faster and he looked away as he worked with the nurse to get Ms. Bayberry to transport.

Mindy made it clear that he was to stick by his patient's side and make sure that she didn't go into pre-term labor. He had to stay focused. He was already in Mindy's bad books, even though he'd made it clear to her that it had been a mistake.

And it had been. A huge mistake.

If only Mindy hadn't been his new boss.

If only what?

Could he honestly tell himself that he wouldn't have pursued her? No, he wouldn't have, because right now he didn't have time for that sort of thing. The only thing about their one night together was he wouldn't have thought it a mistake. Never a mistake.

He wheeled Ms. Bayberry out of the emergency department, with only one glance back to see residents in his class darting through Trauma after their attending, getting their hands dirty, wishing he was working with Dr. Chang on the child she'd been wheeling up to surgery.

A touch from Ms. Bayberry brought him back to the present. The gauze on her forehead was soaked and as they waited on for the elevator to come, he reached down and gingerly touched her forehead.

"Has anyone seen to that?"

"It's just a scratch," she said, but wincing as she did so.

"Let me take a look." As he peeled back the bandages, he could see a large gash. One that would leave a nasty scar but wasn't life-threatening. "That's not pleasant."

"I'm sure it's not," Ms. Bayberry said, her voice rising. "I was more concerned about getting my babies checked out than having them attend to my cut."

"Of course, but I think we'll have someone with real talent stitch that up for you, okay?"

She smiled. "You?"

"No, not me. I'm a pediatric surgeon, I deal with delicate stitches, but we're very fortunate to have a former plastic surgeon to the *stars* on staff."

Ms. Bayberry chuckled and the doors to the elevator opened. Sam stopped an intern who was getting off the elevator.

"Page Dr. Alexander in Plastics to come to the fourth floor OB/GYN ultrasound room. Stat."

The intern looked confused, but nodded.

"You don't have to page a special plastic surgeon to stitch me up, Doctor. I'm sure you can do a fine job."

Sam smiled down at her. "I could do an okay job but, come on, we have to have you looking spiffy when those babies come out and you have your first photographs with them. Wash away any reminder of today."

Ms. Bayberry grinned and leaned back against the pillows as the elevator headed up to the fourth floor. He'd take care of her scars. He just wished all scars were all that easy to wash away.

"Dr. Napier, what is going on in there?" Mindy stood in the doorway of the ultrasound room, watching as a tanned, blond-haired Adonis from the plastic surgical ward was bent over her patient, working on her forehead.

"I'm trying to concentrate here," Dr. Alexander said over his shoulder in an annoyed tone.

Sam rolled his eyes and Mindy could tell there was tension between the two of them.

Who *wasn't* Sam fighting with at this hospital? *Sheesh*. She had been hearing some tales about the so-called lone wolf of the residency program.

After her lengthy discussion with Dr. Hall, Mindy got called to assess on another small case, one that wasn't urgent, but as Sam hadn't paged her that Ms. Bayberry had gone into pre-term labor or that there were unusual findings with her ultrasound, Mindy foolishly trusted Sam was okay.

She did not expect to walk in on one of the top plastic surgeons, working on her patient and in the ultrasound room.

"What is going here, Dr. Napier?" Mindy asked again in hushed undertones as Sam shut the door. "You were supposed to report back to me with the results of Ms. Bayberry's ultrasound."

"You told me not to leave her side. You told me to monitor her for pre-term labor."

Mindy crossed her arms. "Why the heck is Dr.

Alexander in there, stitching up her forehead? I thought her wound was shut with skin glue?"

Sam winced. "I know, but it was going to leave a nasty scar."

"So you thought that putting her through more stress of unnecessary stitching would be better for her? What if she goes into pre-term labor?"

"She won't. The babies are fine and she hasn't been having any contractions or bleeding. I checked her myself."

Mindy cocked an eyebrow. "You checked her yourself?"

"I have done that kind of procedure before."

"Do you really think her having the stitches is a top priority?"

"I do. The babies are stable, for now, but there was an irregularity I need you to look at. I had you paged ten minutes ago, but figured you were with another patient."

Mindy pulled out her pager. "I wasn't paged…" And then trailed off when she saw that she had indeed been paged over ten minutes ago by Sam, but the darned thing was on silent mode.

Dammit.

When she had her private practice, she was only dealing with her patients. She wasn't on a rotation at a hospital. She wasn't called in to deal with traumatic events to pregnant mothers. When she was needed in the hospital it was because she scheduled her time there. She was not used to working in a busy hospital, not used to dealing with trauma patients or residents who were in her service.

She was not off to a good start.

"My apologies, Dr. Napier." The blood rushed to her cheeks.

"There's no need to apologize, Dr. Walker. Now that you're here I'd like to show you the results of Ms. Bayberry's ultrasound."

"Of course." Mindy followed him into the consult room, where they sat down in front of the computer.

Sam brought up the ultrasounds of the twins. "As you can see, there is no fluid or blood pooling anywhere. The placenta is attached and no obvious tears."

"She's lucky. When she was rammed by the car behind her and pushed into the car in front of her the steering-wheel pushed into her abdomen."

"Well, that's it exactly. I know it's not your field of surgery." Sam did some more clicks. "But there's lots of blood in her spleen. I think she's damaged her spleen and it could rupture."

Mindy leaned forward. "I think you're right, Dr. Napier."

Dammit.

Taking a ruptured spleen out of a woman who was not so far into her pregnancy was going to be tricky. Not impossible, but tricky. It could send her patient into pre-term labor and that's not something she wanted.

They needed to keep those babies in utero for as long as possible.

"We're going to need a consult from someone who is used to repairing and or removing spleens in high-pressure situations. Page Dr. Ootaka for a consult."

Sam nodded. "Of course, Dr. Walker."

"Good catch, Sam. Thanks for looking at the bigger picture."

Sam shrugged. "In pediatrics we sometimes have to look at the bigger picture when it comes to kids."

He left the consult room and Mindy leaned back in her chair, but only for a moment. She got up and entered the exam room where Dr. Alexander was just dressing his handiwork.

"There, all done." He grinned down at Ms. Bayberry. "Now, when those babies are born, there won't be any sign of a scar."

"Thank you, Dr. Alexander," Mindy said.

Dr. Alexander shrugged. "Sam's my girl-friend's roommate. It was the least I could do." He collected up his things and left.

Mindy turned to her patient. "Your babies are fine, Ms. Bayberry. There is no sign of injury to your uterus or your placenta. Things with the babies look stable. However, your spleen was damaged in the accident."

"What does that mean?" Ms. Bayberry asked,

her voice rising an octave. The monitors on her alerted Mindy to the up-kick in blood pressure.

"It means we have to go in and repair your spleen." Mindy moved toward the bed. "May I look?"

Ms. Bayberry nodded and Mindy lifted the blanket, to see the bruising on the left side of her abdomen. The patient winced.

"Yes, we need to go and repair the damage," Mindy said gently.

"How are you going to do that?"

"Laparoscopically," Dr. Ootaka said, coming into the room, trailed by two of his residents. "I'm Dr. Takeo Ootaka. I have done this procedure countless times. You are in good hands."

"What about my babies?" Ms. Bayberry asked nervously, her eyes instantly darting to Sam, who stood by the door. She'd obviously latched onto Sam as a bit of a safety blanket, which often happened in traumatic situations.

"Dr. Napier and I will be in the OR the entire time. We'll monitor your babies and make sure they stay right where they belong."

Dr. Ootaka grunted in approval and then turned to the male resident with him. "Prep this woman for a CT and then surgery. May I look?"

Dr. Ootaka didn't wait for permission as he leaned over Ms. Bayberry's left side.

"Yes. Yes. We'll take care of this, Ms. Bayberry," Dr. Ootaka said.

Mindy gave her a reassuring squeeze on the shoulder as Dr. Ootaka's residents began to prep Ms. Bayberry and Mindy walked with Dr. Ootaka to the hall, with Sam trailing behind.

"I plan to have your patient down to the OR in the next hour, maybe less. I don't need to tell you that massive internal bleeding will put those babies in jeopardy."

Mindy nodded. "My resident and I will be ready, scrubbed in and waiting."

Dr. Ootaka nodded. "Good."

"Let's go, Dr. Napier."

"I thought you wanted me to stay with Ms. Bayberry?" Sam asked.

"She's in good hands with Dr. Ootaka's residents. They can monitor her. Right now we have to get a neonatal team ready and on standby in case Ms. Bayberry goes into premature labor."

"You think that will happen?"

"I hope it won't," Mindy said quickly as they moved down the hall to gather their team and ready them for surgery. She stopped and stretched her back, groaning.

"What's wrong?" Sam asked.

"Just a sore spot. It's been a while since I've been on a long rotation in a hospital."

Sam grunted. "What, they don't have long rotations at the hospitals in California?"

"For your information, Dr. Napier, I had a private practice, or did you not hear a word Dr. Chang said when she introduced me?"

"You told me in no uncertain terms that your personal life was not my concern. I'm just your resident." There was a devilish twinkle to his eyes as he said it.

Darn him.

He was proving to be a challenge.

"You're right. I did. So why don't you go back to Ms. Bayberry and continue to monitor her until she's brought down to the OR. Also, make sure her next of kin is updated on the situation."

"Of course, Dr. Walker." Then he did a little bow of his head and headed back to the exam room where Ms. Bayberry was.

Mindy sighed. He was a pain, but he was a good physician. The way he was with Ms. Bayberry, reassuring her, taking care of her.

She'd seen the look of longing when he'd been watching Dr. Chang working on patients. The drive, that look of ambition, she knew it well. When she had been in her obstetrics fellowship she and Dean had worked side by side to gain the attention of one the most noted maternal-fetal specialists on the West Coast, Dr. Guild.

The spark of competition and rivalry. That's what had driven her and Dean closer together, why the attraction had grown. At least, that's what she'd thought. Now she wasn't so sure.

It wasn't competition or rivalry with Sam, but he was trying to show his self-worth. He was trying to prove to her that he was tough, that he didn't have a soft underbelly when it came to his patients.

Or to her.

And then an image of their night together flashed through her mind. Of Sam and her together, his arms around her, his hands in her hair and his lips against her skin. It caused her blood to burn.

Mindy took a deep, calming breath. She couldn't think of Sam that way. He was a resident. She wasn't looking for a relationship. She didn't want one. They were too much trouble.

Sam was here to learn from her. That's all.

And Mindy had to keep telling herself that to get through the rotation, heck, the next week while he was on her service. When he was off her service and back in Peds then there would be a safe, comfortable distance between the two of them.

He was after a pediatric fellowship, not OB/GYN, and she didn't have any room to mentor a fellow. OB/GYN fellows went through Dr. Finn. All she was here for was maternal-fetal medicine and infertility issues. She was here to bring in big cases, to bring in money for West Manhattan Saints.

She was here to rebuild her life and that life didn't include Dr. Sam Napier.

It couldn't.

CHAPTER FOUR

SAM SHOOK HIS head at the nurse in the OR, who was holding up his cellphone again so he could see that it was buzzing. Sam mouthed the words "Not important" and "Scrubbing in" to the nurse, who was annoyed that his phone on the sterile tray was the only one giving her an issue.

He cursed under his breath as the water washed over his arms. He knew exactly what those texts were about.

Darn Langley.

"What's with all the texts? Is it from the woman you slept with last night?" Rebecca asked, as she came up beside him to scrub in.

"What?" Sam snapped.

Rebecca smirked. "Oh, come on. I'm not an

idiot. Holly told me all about you. So who is the woman?"

"I don't know what Holly has been telling you. Whatever it is, it's not true. No one and it's not her."

"Aha, so you admit you got some action."

Sam cursed under his breath. "Would you stop concerning yourself in my personal life?"

"Okay, I didn't mean to tick you off."

Sam rolled his eyes and lathered the soap over his hands. "If you must know, it's my mother. She got wind that I'm on an OB/GYN service this week as a sort of a punishment."

Rebecca frowned. "I wouldn't call working with Dr. Walker a punishment. Have you read some of her papers? She's a big deal."

"I didn't say it was punishment." In fact, it wasn't. He was enjoying his time on Dr. Walker's service, but he knew his mother. Nothing was as worthy or extraordinary as neuro.

Sam rinsed and then shook his hands over the sink. He headed into the OR and was helped into a gown and gloves. He was hoping that they were just a precaution, that they wouldn't have to be used to deliver the twins.

Out of the corner of his eyes he could see the neonatologist team, ready and waiting. Then he saw Mindy, attaching the monitors and watching as the babies' heartbeats came online.

Please, let them stay in.

He knew the survival rate for infants so young was low.

"Dr. Napier?" a small voice called out to him.

Sam went over to Ms. Bayberry's side. She was trembling, waiting for anesthesia, her arms strapped down.

"I'm here," he said.

There was relief. "I'm glad you're here."

"Of course. Where else would I be?"

Ms. Bayberry smiled. "How are the babies?"

Sam glanced over at Mindy and the monitors. Mindy nodded and gave a thumbs-up.

"They're doing really good, Ms. Bayberry."

"Please, just call me Linda. I feel like an old lady when you call me that."

Sam chuckled. "Deal. As long as you call me Sam, then."

"Sam?" she said. "I would've never pegged you for a Sam. I thought you were Scottish."

"I'm American too." He winked.

"Is my husband on his way?" she asked.

"He's in the waiting room. I'll give him regular updates, I promise." Sam glanced up as Dr. Ootaka entered the OR, with Rebecca trailing him. "I think they're going to get started soon. I'm going to watch those babies like a hawk. I won't let them out of my sight."

Linda sighed and nodded, staring back up at the ceiling.

Sam stepped out of the way of the anesthesiologist and glanced up in the gallery. He could see Holly amongst the crowd of eager onlookers. Whenever Dr. Ootaka did a surgery he always garnered a lot of attention. Enzo and Kimberlyn would've been all over this. He missed them.

The room was filled with some of West Manhattan Saints' finest surgeons.

His mother should be pleased with that, instead of harassing him with endless texts about wasting his time when he should be focusing on pediatrics. And if he'd changed his mind about pediatrics then he shouldn't be *slumming* in OB/GYN when he could switch over to neuro. She could pull some strings.

Even though he hadn't read the texts, he knew exactly what they said, because they were always the same.

Always. It annoyed him. As if he wanted her help. Sam didn't want anything from her.

At least that was one thing his mother had going for her; she was a creature of habit.

Sam moved toward Mindy as Linda drifted off and they put the tube down her throat. Sam watched the monitor closely, keeping his distance.

"She can't be under too long, Dr. Ootaka," Mindy piped up as she took her seat next to the fetal monitor. The steady sound of the two heartbeats beat in time with his own.

"I'm well aware of that, Dr. Walker. Ten blade."

The surgery began as laparoscopic incisions

were made and the camera inserted to get a better look at the damage done to the spleen.

"You should really move closer," Mindy whispered. "You could learn a lot from Dr. Ootaka."

"I'm fine right here, Dr. Walker." Sam eyed the monitor as the heartbeat of twin A began to rise, but just slightly.

"Are you sure?" Mindy asked.

"I promised her that I wouldn't take my eyes off the babies. Even if it means they're still inside her."

"Okay, then." There was a hint of admiration in her voice and it secretly pleased him that he had impressed her.

Don't think about that.

All eyes in the gallery were focused on Dr. Ootaka and his team.

"Do you know what injection I gave Ms. Bayberry before we came in here?" Mindy asked casually.

"Is this a test?" Sam asked confused.

"Sort of. Just passing some time. So do you?"

"Since the risk of pre-term labor is high I

would *hope* that you injected some corticosteroids into her, thus speeding along lung development of the babies."

"Correct, Dr. Napier."

"I've dealt with preemies before, Dr. Walker. I do work in pediatrics."

"What about a micro-preemie? Have you ever delivered or worked on a micro-preemie before?"

Sam grinned behind his mask. He could never forget Maya, who was Enzo's niece. He had been there when she'd come in. She had been his charge and he'd made it his personal mission to take care of her. Maya was alive because of him. "I have. In my first year."

"You've seen a lot, then," Mindy remarked.

"I have, and I hope to see more when I gain a fellowship spot with Dr. Chang."

"No disrespect to Dr. Chang, but she's not a neonatologist. If you want to work with preemies you should be working with Dr. Hall in the NICU."

"Dr. Hall is a great surgeon, but I need a peds fellowship before I move into neonatology. Like you, I want many feathers in my cap."

"You're very sure of yourself."

Sam didn't respond. They'd had this discussion before and it didn't bother him that she thought of him that way. In surgery that was a compliment. Suddenly an alarm went off and Mindy leapt to her feet.

"Dr. Walker, what is going on down there?" Dr. Ootaka demanded. "This is a delicate procedure."

"I am well aware of that, Dr. Ootaka," Mindy snapped. "One of the twins is distressed."

"Is she in labor?"

Mindy shook her head. "No. Just the baby being active and jostling around."

The general surgical team had stopped what they were doing so as not cause any more damage by the moving baby and because of that Linda's blood pressure went down.

"Dammit," Mindy cursed under her breath. "We have to get that baby to calm down. If it doesn't, I'll have to deliver or risk the mother bleeding out because they can't repair her spleen."

Sam thought back to when his stepmother had been pregnant with twins. The boys had been active and the only way his father had been able to get them to settle down had been to talk to them softly, in a deep, even voice.

"Let me try." Sam stepped forward and placed his hands on Linda's belly. Leaning over, he began to recite an old Gaelic song his father used to sing to his brothers. He was very aware that all eyes were on him and that everyone was listening to him sing, but he didn't care.

He'd made a promise to Linda Bayberry. It was better if the babies stayed in utero.

The alarms disappeared, the jostling settled and the babies were no longer a threat to their mother's spleen removal.

"Whatever you're doing, Dr. Napier, keep it up," Dr. Ootaka said. "It's unconventional, but it works and that's the most important thing."

It was a compliment and Sam took it and continued singing, his hands on the side of Linda's abdomen where the more restless twin was. As if in appreciation of his singing, a gentle kick nudged his palm, reminding him why he did what he did in the first place.

Mindy smiled as she watched Mr. Bayberry lean over and kiss the top of Linda's head, his hand on her belly. Linda was still groggy and missing her spleen, but the babies were okay, though Mindy had every intention of keeping Linda in the hospital for some time to monitor her, especially since she'd had a major organ removed.

It was touch and go, especially when that one twin had started acting up and then Sam had stepped up and calmed the fetus down. As if the fetus had known the mother trusted him.

He'd sung to the babies. Calming them and melting her heart.

Would Dean ever have done that? She seriously doubted it.

Sam might put up barriers to keep people out, but he had such a soft spot, especially when it came to children, and for her that was something that was highly attractive in a man.

Dammit.

Mindy shook her head and headed down to the cafeteria to get something to eat. It was late at night so really she should just head for home, but she wanted to stay and monitor Ms. Bayberry through the night.

The cafeteria had limited service so late, but at least she could get a sandwich from a machine and coffee. When she entered the dimly lit cafeteria there was one other soul there, hunched over a table, eating a pathetic-looking sandwich and nursing what looked like a generic can of diet soda.

Walk away.

Only she couldn't, because she was a weak fool. "You did good in there today."

Sam looked up. "Dr. Walker? I thought your shift was over?"

"I could say the same thing about yours as well, Dr. Napier."

Sam shrugged. "I made a promise. I'm going to stay here and monitor her for the night."

"Funny, that's what I thought I was going to do."

Sam cocked an eyebrow. "An attending? Usually attendings fob those kinds of jobs off on us lowly residents or even lower interns."

Mindy chuckled. "Mind if I join you?"

"No, not at all."

Mindy sank down into the hard plastic chair and let out a sigh of relief. She hadn't realized how long she'd been standing.

"Is the patient's husband with her?"

Mindy nodded. "He is. She's still quite groggy, but in stable condition."

"Good. Are you planning on keeping her in the hospital for a while?"

"Yep. She needs to heal. She's had major surgery and is pregnant with twins, which adds an extra burden on the body. I'll probably keep her here until those babies are ready to be born."

"That's a long time."

Mindy shrugged. "The protein in her blood was a little high for my liking and as I gave her an injection of cortocosteriods the chances that she could develop pre-eclampsia are slightly higher now. I'd rather have her here, where I can watch her."

"Now, that I didn't know," Sam remarked, as he slid the uneaten half of his sandwich toward her.

"What?" Mindy asked, gladly taking the sandwich.

"The risk of pre-eclampsia and the ACS."

"Any time you give a pregnant woman a drug it's risky. When you add the stress of twins, well..." Mindy trailed off. "We'll keep an eye on her."

"I will. You should go home and sleep. You look like you didn't get much sleep last night." And then he winked, causing her to blush.

"That was inappropriate, Dr. Napier."

"I'm sorry. I couldn't resist. When I get tired I get a little punchy and, besides, you're eating my sandwich."

Mindy chuckled. "It's terrible."

Sam shrugged. "It's nutrition, sort of. I lived off vending-machine sandwiches as a kid."

"Really? How random."

Sam shrugged. "It is what it is."

"You should go home, Sam. That's an order."

He cocked an eyebrow. "Are we on a first-name basis now?"

No, they weren't. Not since they'd spent the night together, which had been last night. She'd made it clear that she didn't trust him, that their one night of passion was to be forgotten. It had never happened.

Yet, sitting here with him in an empty cafeteria after a stressful surgery, worrying about whether or not they would have to deliver two babies who probably wouldn't make it, caused her to let her guard down.

"What was that song you were singing?" she asked, changing the subject.

Sam chuckled and then ran his fingers through his hair. "It was *'Huis, Huis air an Each'*. Just a simple song my father would sing to my twin brothers. It used to calm them, thought I would give it a shot. I'm actually surprised I remembered the words."

"It was beautiful. Wish I knew the words."

Sam smiled, those blue eyes twinkling in the

dim light, and then the smile faded and he looked away. "Well, I'm glad it worked."

"Me too." Mindy swallowed the last of the sandwich, which stuck in her throat as silence descended between them. "Well, I'd better go check on Ms. Bayberry."

Sam shook his head. "Go home. I'll round on her tonight."

"Don't you have a home to go to?"

"It's just a flat in a brownstone overrun by other surgeons. Most will be here tonight anyhow, and I don't fancy riding the subway back to Brooklyn tonight."

Mindy nodded. "Well, make sure you get some sleep tonight. I'll be starting my rounds at six in the morning."

Sam nodded. "I'll be there. Goodnight, Dr. Walker."

"Goodnight, Dr. Napier."

Mindy got up and hurried out of the cafeteria, not looking back even though she could feel his gaze on her, watching her walk away.

This was going to be difficult. Everything

about him drew her in—the compassion he had for his patients, his talent, the air of mystery about him.

He's off-limits.

And she had to keep telling herself that. She had to keep reminding herself that Sam was off-limits. She was his teacher.

Not that there was a specific rule about attendings, residents and interns, but it would be detrimental to Sam's career if people thought he was sleeping his way to the top. She should know, rumors had spread about her. After word had got out about Dean and Owen, the two people she'd trusted and worked in partnership with, it had destroyed her reputation in one fell swoop.

How could a patient put faith in someone who had put their faith in the hands of people who had duped her for so long?

Words and knowledge had power. If used by the wrong people, it could destroy everything Sam had worked for and she didn't want that for him. If today was any indication Mindy had no doubt that Sam was going to be a brilliant pediatric surgeon and she wasn't going to let a rumor about the two of them destroy that.

So she had to be careful about how she addressed him.

She couldn't let herself slip into familiarity.

She had to keep her distance from him and not get sucked in by the spell he seemed to be able to cast over her. She was made of stronger stuff than that; at least she thought she was. Although Dean and Owen had lied to her for so long, so what did she know?

Mindy stopped and glanced back over her shoulder down the hall toward the cafeteria, but Sam had disappeared. Probably he was on his way to check on Ms. Bayberry.

Go home before you do or say something you'll regret.

Mindy sighed and headed toward the attendings' lounge to change into her street clothes. It had been her first major rotation since starting at West Manhattan Saints. She was exhausted, but she also didn't want to go home. Her apartment was empty, lonely and memories of Sam were everywhere.

Don't chicken out. Go home.

Mindy groaned and tried not to think about what had taken place at her apartment last night, in her bed, because those thoughts, though pleasant, were very unwelcome and for a moment she was terrified she wasn't going to be able to succeed in keeping her distance from him.

She was pretty darned sure that she was going to fail miserably, but what a way to fail.

CHAPTER FIVE

SAM HAD BEEN off Mindy's rotation for two weeks and he found he missed it, but she had to give a fair shake to other residents applying for the fellowship. His first week back on the peds round he happened upon Dr. Snow, who was currently on rotation with Mindy, and all she was doing was whining about how nasty and how hard it was.

How the patients whined and complained constantly.

As if kids didn't whine?

Sam laughed to himself as he thought of that. When he'd worked his full week with Mindy he'd learned so much. She'd kept her distance since she'd accidentally called him Sam after Ms. Bayberry's surgery, but that was fine by him.

He didn't want rumors starting.

It was bad enough having a famous mother, one who had slept with the current chief of surgery, albeit twenty years ago. He'd told Enzo about it when they'd got to know each other, but he was the only other person who knew, besides Dr. Chang, who knew his mother as well from medical school. And Sam didn't have to worry about anyone accusing him of favoritism when it came to his mother and Dr. Amelia Chang.

It was no secret that his mother and Dr. Chang did not see eye to eye. Sam had actually been concerned when he'd first been accepted into the surgical residency program. He'd known that he'd always wanted to be a pediatric surgeon. He loved working with kids, but when he'd heard the head of Pediatrics was his mother's "nemesis" of sorts, he had been worried that he wouldn't have a shot in heck of getting into the program, but he'd applied anyway.

And had been accepted.

Dr. Chang had known exactly who he was. She had told him as much on the first day he'd become a resident and had started clocking hours on the peds floor.

He'd been charting when she'd come up beside him.

"You have your mother's eyes."

"Pardon me?"

She stared at him, those thoughtful obsidian eyes boring right through him. "You have your father's soul. Let's hope you have your mother's talent. If you do, you'll be brilliant."

That was all she'd said. She would request him at odd intervals and always with the most delicate situations or the toughest cases.

Dr. Chang would observe him.

It's why he and Enzo had become more than just competition in their first year of residency. They'd moved beyond the macho chest-thrusting and territory-marking in the game of surgery and had become friends, because Sam had been there when Enzo's niece Maya had been born.

Dr. Chang had put Maya, a fragile preemie with a low expectation to survive, in his charge. And Maya had thrived because Sam had known that a way to help regulate a heartbeat was to place the baby against a bare chest. It was called kangaroo care. Maya hadn't been able to feed and Enzo's sister had been unable at that point to provide skin to skin contact, so during a long shift at night Sam had sat down in a rocking chair in the NICU and had done just that for little Maya. Wrapping her up against his chest, upright and prone, cradled on the inside of his scrubs, a blanket over them while he'd charted, very poorly.

Enzo had caught him, pausing slightly in the doorway of the NICU. He hadn't teased him, hadn't said anything. A look had been all that was needed to understand what was happening.

It was because of that he'd had a permanent spot at Enzo's family home for dinner and when he hadn't shown up, plates of food had been sent to him.

Sam chuckled and leaned over his chart. He missed Enzo. Missed seeing him in the halls of West Manhattan Saints. He missed the food.

Darn him for falling in love with Kimberlyn and them moving away.

It had gotten him through some lonely patches when he'd first moved to New York. His mother didn't have much to do with him and the rest of his close family was in Scotland. His dad, his brothers and stepmother, as well as various aunts, uncles, cousins and one venerable grand-mother.

Even though he'd been born in New York and had spent some time on this side of the pond, he was alone. When he'd been with his mother, he'd been alone. She had always been working and he'd spent a lot of his childhood, when he'd been with her, in the hallways of the hospital or in the observation room while she'd been in surgery.

He glanced up from his charting and saw Mindy in the NICU, bending over a tiny mi-cro-preemie in an incubator. Mindy was in her scrubs and updating the neonatologist so it ap-peared that the baby had just been born.

She's alone.

Mindy had said she'd grown up on the west

coast, a native to California. Though she hadn't moved an ocean away from her family, she'd moved clear across the country to start a new life. It must've been something drastic that had chased her away. To isolate herself.

He didn't know about isolating oneself on purpose, but he did get loneliness. Even living in a house full of other surgeons. Tessa had moved out and was starting a family, Kimberlyn and Enzo were together and gone, even Holly had moved on with Dr. Alexander and she had family around. Sure, there was the new roommate, Rebecca, but he didn't really know her yet and wasn't sure he wanted to. She was too chatty.

He had no one. Just like Mindy didn't have anyone and he felt sorry for her. She deserved better and though he shouldn't approach her, he should just keep his distance from her, he closed his chart and headed toward the NICU.

Mindy was standing next to the incubator, staring down at the small preemie inside, but he could tell by her expression that she really wasn't watching the preemie. She had a far-off expression on her face.

"Boy or girl?" Sam asked, as he came up beside her and peered down at the bundle, hooked up to wires but alive.

"Boy," Mindy said offhandedly. She set down the chart she was holding. "I delivered him about an hour ago after I repaired his CPAM."

"Congenital pulmonary airway malformation?"

"Yes. I usually try to keep the fetus inside after I do the repair, but Mom had the beginning stages of pre-eclampsia. With the extra stressors of surgery, I delivered the baby."

"Wish I could have seen that procedure in action."

Mindy cocked any eyebrow. "I thought that maternal-fetal medicine wasn't your intended specialty, that your main focus was pediatrics?"

"It is, but it doesn't mean I don't appreciate complex surgeries. Especially when those complex surgeries involve children. Perhaps I judged maternal-fetal medicine too harshly."

"Really now?" she asked, obviously humored.

Sam leaned over and gazed at the lad through the glass. "Poor mite."

"Yes, it was unfortunate, but now that it's repaired he has a shot of growing up normally. Of surviving. Twenty or thirty years ago he wouldn't have survived his birth."

"Is this where you're going to start spouting off at me about how my chosen specialty is for dinosaurs?" Sam teased. "That there will be no need for pediatric surgeons or neonatologists?"

Mindy laughed. "I'm sorry, Dr. Napier. As I said, I was quite annoyed to see you as a resident."

"I know. I know. Trust me, I felt the same."

"You were annoyed I was an attending?"

Sam nodded. "Of course. A woman I'd had an amazing night with was now off-limits."

Mindy snorted. "Like you had every intention of calling me again." She walked out of the NICU and Sam trailed after her.

"You don't know that," Sam protested. Though she was right. At the time he hadn't had any intention of calling her again, but spending a week with her on her service had made him think differently about her. He'd seen her in a new light. If it wasn't a bad idea, if he had more time to commit to a relationship instead of being tied to the hospital, he would pursue a woman like Mindy Walker.

"We didn't exchange numbers," Mindy said.

"Ah, but I know where you live. I could've found out if I chose too."

Mindy chuckled. "That sounds mighty stalkerish, Dr. Napier. Mighty stalkerish indeed."

Sam groaned. "Oh, come on. It's not stalkerish at all." He leaned over the charge desk as she pulled a chart from behind the counter. "How is the new resident on your service going?"

"That's not any of your business," Mindy said, not looking at him.

"I'm just curious, that's all."

"No, you're not. You're competitive, you shark." It wasn't said in an accusatory tone, there was a twinkle to her eyes.

"I swear, it's not competitive in nature. Just curious. I heard some…complaints."

Mindy's mouth dropped open. "Complaints? What do you mean, complaints? From who?"

Sam grinned. "I can't say, unless I want to get attacked by a pod of sharks. Do sharks come in pods, I wonder?"

Mindy frowned and then playfully pushed. "Jerk!"

"What was that for?"

"What complaints?" Mindy demanded. "As your superior, I demand you tell me."

Sam cocked an eyebrow. "As my superior, you demand I tell you? I don't think so." He turned to leave but she grabbed his arm.

"Come on, tell me. This is my first job in a teaching hospital and I want to make sure that I'm imparting my wisdom on the residents well."

"You're doing a fine job. Really, the complaints were that you were a bit demanding and a workhorse."

Mindy smiled then, but then cleared her throat. "Is that all?"

"It pleases you to know you're being tough."

"It does. I want them to be afraid of me and my service."

"You want to be like the Godzilla of the OB/GYN floor?" Sam asked.

"If you can survive my toughness then you can make it in my field."

"Ah, but there's a problem. The residents currently rotating on your service aren't OB/GYN residents. You have a whole smackerel of them who are chomping at the bit to work with you. You're working with residents who are eyeing a pediatric fellowship with Dr. Chang. So it might be lost on them."

Mindy smiled smugly. "That may be, Dr. Napier, but I deal with kids when they're still developing. I have to be hard on all residents who have any kind of inkling of wanting to work with children. They're a precious commodity. If you can't stand the heat..."

"Get out of the oven?"

Mindy laughed. "Kitchen, Dr. Napier."

"So, I have to ask, did Dr. Snow do well in the procedure?"

"I wouldn't know. She never did make it to surgery."

Sam was confused. "I can't see her missing something like that. She'd as soon as skin me than let me have a shot at any specialized procedure. Of all the sharks, she's the nastiest."

"You think highly of her," Mindy teased, and then she sighed. "Actually, I didn't let her into my OR and she's effectively off my service."

Now he was intrigued. "And you're not going to elaborate any further."

"It's not prudent. You are her competition."

Sam didn't say anything further as Mindy finished her charting and set the binder back in its place. The only thing that would have kept Dr. Snow out of surgery was if she'd done something really bad to anger her attending. In their first days, Dr. Snow had been a bit pompous, but she was a talented surgeon and Sam couldn't help but wonder what Dr. Snow had done. Well, whatever it was, it wasn't his business to know.

Mindy was right. Dr. Snow was his competition and he didn't want to have any unfair advantages.

"That's foolish, Samuel! Take whatever advantages you can get. Given the chance, another surgeon will stab you in the back to take your spot."

His mother's cutthroat attitude had never sat well with him.

It was his father's gentle soul which always seemed to win out. His mother's downfall was that sometimes she acted before she thought and Sam was a bit more methodical. He didn't gossip; he didn't jump into the fray unless it was during a medical emergency.

"I'm going to go grab a coffee. I still have a few more hours left on my shift. I'll see you around." Mindy moved around to the other side of the charge desk and headed down the hall.

"Dr. Walker... Mindy, wait."

Mindy spun around, stunned, but she didn't chastise him for using her first name.

"Would you like to get a cup of coffee with

me? I'm on call, but I thought you might like some company."

What are you doing?

He didn't know. He never acted this spontaneously, but he couldn't help himself. All he knew was he was probably setting himself up for something he wasn't sure he was ready for.

Mindy stood there for a few moments, absolutely dumbfounded. It felt like she was standing there for hours, but of course that was foolish.

She was surprised that Sam had asked her to have coffee with him.

Say no. You can't trust him. He's just using you.

"Sure." She couldn't believe the words that were coming out of her mouth.

What're you doing? She didn't know at that moment. She was actually surprised at herself, but she was lonely. She knew hardly anyone in New York. There was no harm in getting a cup of coffee.

Sam smiled the grin that melted her heart. *Darn him.*

"Good. I have to get my post-op notes off to Dr. Chang. I'll meet you in the cafeteria in thirty minutes?"

"No, not the cafeteria." If she was going to go through with this then she was going to do it outside the hospital.

"Where, then? I'm on call and I can't go far."

"There's a coffee shop next to the hospital. You'll be close enough to run back if you get called in."

"Okay." Sam picked up his notes. "I'll see you there in half an hour."

"Sure," she said nervously, and then quickly walked away before she did something ridiculous like blush.

This was not going according to plan. Her plan had been to swear off Sam, even though she knew that was going to be a hard thing to do. There were so many things about him that she liked and admired. She also had a hard time forgetting about the way he kissed, even though that had been nearly a month ago.

Sam was also the only person she'd really connected with in New York. She'd spoken to other attendings, her patients, nurses, but there wasn't a connection. Mindy had been so busy she hadn't had the time to form any friendships or to get to know anyone. And she had a hard time opening up.

Perhaps she was blocking them out because she was scared of trusting people. Especially after what had happened in California.

She'd been deceived and she'd had no idea. Instead she'd lived in this oblivious little bubble, thinking that her marriage was okay, that her best friend wasn't betraying her. All the things she'd told Owen made her stomach knot. She'd been such a fool.

After it had all gone down it had been the pitying looks she'd been unable to handle. The "Poor Mindy"'s. She hadn't liked being pitied. When she'd been an intern she'd struggled that first year and had been pitied. She'd been the underdog and scared of her own shadow.

When Dr. Guild had taken her under her wing Mindy had blossomed. That shy girl who had dominated her life had disappeared and all of those who had dubbed her the runt of the surgical litter had been left behind as she'd become a surgical star.

It was hard for Mindy to make friends. She just didn't want to open herself up to any more hurt.

With Sam it was totally different. She was just at ease around him. She liked to talk to him and she kept forgetting that she shouldn't be so relaxed around him, because Sam was off-limits and because she refused to open her heart again. It just wasn't worth it.

She found herself in the coffee shop next to the hospital, still in a bit of daze, with a latte in her hand. One of those limited edition spiced ones.

Mindy took a seat in the corner, waiting with anticipation for Sam to come. Though part of her hoped he wouldn't. It would be easier if he didn't show and she was hoping that he would be called to something.

The chime over the door tingled and Sam walked in. He didn't see her at first, so she watched as every female in the coffee shop turned their appreciative gaze on him and she had to admit she couldn't blame them. He was tall, broad-shouldered, with dark reddish hair, ridiculously gorgeous features and eyes that had no business being on a man who wasn't going to be an actor or a model.

Mindy could almost see him in a kilt with a big giant sword. What do the Highlanders call their big giant swords?

Why the heck are you thinking about big giant swords at this moment?

Mindy shook her head and rubbed her eyes. She needed to get some more sleep. He ordered a small coffee and headed over to her. All eyes followed the handsome doctor as he slid into the booth across from her.

Sam frowned. "What?"

"What?" Mindy asked, confused.

"You're staring at me like I have horns growing out of my head or something."

"Sorry, I was just watching all your admirers give me the look of death."

Sam glanced over his shoulder and a few female patrons who were still looking in their direction looked away quickly.

Sam chuckled and smiled with smug satisfaction. "Oh, that. I'm used to that."

Mindy snorted. "I'm sure you are. What're you drinking?"

"Black coffee with a shot of espresso. Dr. Chang paged me just as I was leaving. There's a surgery in about thirty minutes."

"Oh?"

Sam nodded. "Not pleasant, I'm afraid, but it needs to be done and once it's done the child will be better off for it."

Mindy was just about to ask what surgery when she got a page herself. She frowned when she saw it was from the OB/GYN department.

It was in regard to Ms. Bayberry. She was

over the crucial twenty-five weeks, but the babies needed longer in utero.

"What's wrong?" Sam asked, as they both stood up together.

"It's Ms. Bayberry." Mindy slipped her phone back into her pocket.

"Is she in labor?" He was concerned. She could tell. Mindy knew he still checked on Linda. It was sweet.

It wasn't just sweet, it was the mark of a caring surgeon. One who was looking beyond being just a surgical god and being an actual *good* doctor. Even if Sam didn't want to admit it. To admit something like that, to admit to caring while in competition with other interns could be a sign of weakness. She should know. Mindy had felt that bite, that sting against her jugular when she cared too deeply, but once she'd realized it didn't matter she no longer cared.

She was going to be the physician she wanted to be and that was all that mattered. Sam was just starting a surgical career. He'd learn it soon enough, but then again maybe he already had and if he did it was commendable. Being a surgical resident was tough. It was supposed to be tough and it was a phase in her life she was glad was over.

"No, she's not in labor." Mindy finished the rest of her latte and crumpled the cup, tossing it into the garbage. "The neonatologist called me. There's something on the ultrasound she wants me to take a look at."

Sam frowned. "Can I come?"

"Don't you have a surgery with Dr. Chang?"

"Not for thirty minutes. If she needs me before then, she can page me. I would really like to be there when you look over the ultrasound."

Mindy grinned. "Changing your mind about maternal-fetal medicine?"

"No." Sam downed the rest of his coffee. "I still want to be a pediatric surgeon, but perhaps after completing my fellowship with Dr. Chang I'll be looking to add maternal-fetal medicine to my résumé. Really specialize."

Mindy cocked an eyebrow. "Wow. You have mighty big aspirations and you're cocky. What makes you think you have a shot at that pediatric fellowship?"

Sam shrugged as they walked out of the coffee house together. "Because I want it and because I'm going to earn it all on my own merit. You said so yourself, I'm a fine surgeon."

"Hmm. That remains to be seen. I haven't actually seen you in any complicated procedure yet."

"That's true. The week I was on your rotation all I did was observe and calm down a set of twins during a splenectomy."

"Maybe I'll have to observe your surgery later with Dr. Chang."

"Or, if there is something that has to be done surgically to Ms. Bayberry's twins, I can be on the case."

"You're pushy," Mindy teased.

"It's only natural. I was the first doctor on her case and she likes me. We have a rapport."

"That's true. I'll think about it."

"It makes the most sense since you've banished Dr. Snow from your service."

Mindy shook her head and they headed to meet Dr. Hall, the neonatologist, in an exam room. When they got there Dr. Hall was frowning as she leaned over the ultrasound image on the computer. She barely glanced over her shoulder to acknowledge them as they walked into the room.

"What seems to be the trouble?" Mindy asked, as she took a seat next to Dr. Hall. Sam stood behind her, leaning over so he could look at the screen as well. She was very aware that he was so close. The heat of his body permeated her scrubs, causing her blood to sing.

"Take a look. It was missed in the ultrasound done by her regular OB/GYN, but now that she's almost thirty weeks you can see it clearly as the twins are in a different position."

Mindy's heart skipped a beat when she saw one of the most rare pregnancy conditions.

"Is that the same amniotic sac?" Sam asked, his breath on her neck.

Mindy moved close to the computer, more to

get away from Sam being so close to her. "Yes, it's a mono-amniotic pregnancy."

"Why was this missed earlier, Dr. Walker?" Sam asked.

"It's sometimes hard to see, depending on where the babies lie." Mindy clicked on a file and brought up an earlier ultrasound, zooming in. "See this line. It looks like it was a membrane dividing the fetuses, but it clearly is not. As they've moved and grown, you can clearly see that no membrane divides the amniotic sac."

"And you can see here, the cords are starting to tangle," Dr. Hall remarked.

Mindy pinched the bridge of her nose. "That's not good."

"No, the babies are at risk of cutting off their blood supply now. Is that correct, Dr. Walker?" Sam asked.

"Yes." Mindy stood. "Ms. Bayberry is thirty weeks tomorrow. We'll have to keep a close eye on her. Let's try to get her to thirty weeks and then we'll deliver the babies."

Dr. Hall nodded. "I'll prep my neonatology staff."

Mindy turned to Sam. "Can you inform Dr. Chang for me, Dr. Napier? I would like her present at the surgery."

"Of course, Dr. Walker." Sam left the room to track down Dr. Chang before she got prepped for surgery.

Dr. Hall left the exam room to prep her team and now Mindy was faced with breaking the news to Ms. Bayberry. As if the poor woman hadn't been under enough stress. Now Mindy had to break the news to her that her twins' lives were in danger. At least when she'd had the splenectomy they'd given Ms. Bayberry a shot of corticosteroids to help strengthen the babies' lungs. She'd be given another shot tonight.

Any little bit helped.

At least the babies were almost thirty weeks.

At least their cords weren't tangling at twenty weeks, when there would be nothing they could do to save them.

Being thirty weeks along, at least the babies had a chance.

And Mindy was going to make sure they got the chance they deserved.

CHAPTER SIX

SAM STOOD NEXT to Dr. Chang as she scrubbed in. He was annoyed that he wasn't going to be allowed into the OR while they delivered Ms. Bayberry's twins.

"There will be too many people in there. It's a delicate surgery, and we have Neonatology, Pediatrics and OB/GYN. You can watch from the gallery, like the other residents."

That command had come down from Professor Langley, but he didn't actually have the guts to come down and tell him in person. He'd sent his lackey to tell him. Langley never really dealt with him. He always seemed to avoid him.

He must feel guilty and that pleased Sam to no end.

Good. Langley's affair with his mother had

torn his family apart. Crushed his father. It was best Langley keep his distance from him.

"You're scowling," Dr. Chang remarked, as she scrubbed her arms and hands.

"I think I should be in there. I was on this case since day one," Sam snapped.

"Professor Langley has a point. There will be a lot of people in there."

"I calmed the patient."

"Yes, when her husband was absent, and she'll be under general anesthesia again. This is a delicate procedure. We can't have the cords continue to tangle. If they tangle before the babies are ready to be born, it could kill both of them."

Sam grunted in response. He got that, but he still wanted to be in there. Mono-amniotic twins was such a rare occurrence he doubted he'd ever get to see another case like this in the near future. In fact, it was Dr. Chang's first time to see such a case. Even she'd never seen mono-amniotic twins.

And it wasn't just the rarity of the case he was moaning about. He cared for the patient. Linda

Bayberry and her husband Frank were two of the nicest native New Yorkers he'd ever met, besides Enzo's family, though he wouldn't let anyone else know that.

He'd been following the case since day one and he wanted to see it through. He wanted to make sure those babies were okay.

"I heard from your mother today," Dr. Chang said, with a note of derision in her tone.

Oh, bloody hell.

"Aye, and what did she want?" His brogue was slipping out in his annoyance.

Dr. Chang smiled at him. "Oh, she wanted to tell me that I'm wasting her son's talent and surgical skill by having him work in OB/GYN. She didn't pay for your education and pull strings for you to be delivering babies like some glorified midwife."

Sam cursed under his breath. "And what would she know about that? I'm sorry she laid into you like that, Dr. Chang. I hope you know that I don't think that way."

Dr. Chang shook off her hands. "I know and I know your mother."

"What did you say to her?"

"Nothing. I hung up on her." There was an evil grin on Dr. Chang's face as she walked into the OR.

Sam chuckled to himself. He was glad that Dr. Chang didn't put up with his mother's ridiculous behavior. He was also angry that his mother had done that. She was bound and determined to ruin his career as a pediatric surgeon.

His mother wouldn't be happy unless he was a bloody neurosurgeon. Not that there was anything wrong with neurosurgeons. On the contrary, he respected many of them—the brain was a delicate organ.

It took such precision to operate on it and the nervous system, but was it any more difficult or delicate than when you were dealing with a heart no bigger than a grape or veins the size of a human hair?

No. It wasn't, but then kids had never really mattered to his mother.

Sam knew all about that.

Disgusted with her behavior, he headed up to the gallery and pushed his way to the front through the throng of eager observers so he could watch Mindy in action.

He was surprised that none of his other room-mates were in the room, but they were probably off doing surgeries, while he was stuck up in the gallery like a first-year intern. Observing, rather than helping.

"Did you hear that Dr. Monica Hanley is com-ing to West Manhattan Saints?"

"No, I hadn't. Get out of town. *The* Dr. Han-ley is coming here. When?"

Sam perked up at the mention of his mother's name and when he glanced around he could see it was two young interns on the other side of the gallery who were talking about it.

"She's coming in a couple of weeks. Appar-ently there's a kid with some kind of inoper-able brain tumor, but she's going to be testing her new surgical procedure to remove the tumor and she's going to do her ground-breaking surgery here."

"That's amazing."

Sam groaned inwardly.

Great. Just what he needed to hear. His mother was coming to West Manhattan Saints to flaunt neurosurgery in his face once again and he was ticked off. Why did she have to come here to do the surgery? Why hadn't Dr. Chang told him his mother was coming? Did Dr. Chang even know? Perhaps she didn't as she'd hung up on her.

Even then, he wouldn't put it past his mother to go over the head of the Pediatrics attending to Professor Langley to get permission to do the surgery here.

Why here?

"I hear her son works at West Manhattan Saints and that's why she's coming." This was said in a hushed undertone.

"Her son? She has a son and he works here? Who is he?"

"I don't know, but I'm sure he's going to get picked to assist. I mean, come on, the son of Dr.

Hanley. I'm sure she pulled strings to get him into the program. He's probably riding on her coattails and doesn't have to lift a finger. Just has all the most awesome surgeries handed to him."

"I hate him on principle," the other intern griped.

Sam's stomach knotted, his worst fears about being his mother's son realized. It was a good thing they had different surnames. This was why he didn't want people to know who his mother was. They would stop looking at him as a surgeon and only see him as someone who'd got to where he was because of his mother.

He wanted to get up and leave, or confront the two gossiping fools as they continued to gossip about Dr. Hanley's son and how crummy a surgeon he was, but instead he blocked them out. He was safe behind his walls.

Sam was here to learn. He was here to observe a once-in-a-lifetime surgery. He was here to advance his career because he was a surgeon. A good surgeon.

He knew one thing—he was *not* going to be

around when his mother was here. He wasn't going to allow that can of worms to taint his surgical career in the hospital where he planned to spend many years becoming one of the best pediatric surgeons. If she was going to be here, he wasn't.

Mindy was still on a high after safely delivering the mono-amniotic twins. This was her third delivery of mono-amniotic twins and thankfully the second successful delivery. In the first year of her fellowship Dr. Guild had delivered a pair, but sadly the cord restriction had been so bad that one twin hadn't made it.

It had crushed Mindy, breaking her heart. She'd almost walked away from maternal-fetal medicine. Who needed that kind of heartbreak every day? But Dr. Guild had talked some sense into her.

"Next time we catch it sooner. Next time we perfect the skill, so that next time we save a life before the life needs to be saved."

Mindy hadn't been able to walk away from

her specialty then. She'd thrown herself into it, because the more she'd learned, the better she'd got and the more lives she'd saved.

Life was short sometimes and it sucked, but that's what drove Mindy to rise above that. To find another way to save more lives.

It's why she had one of the lowest mortality rates for a surgeon who was so young.

Saving lives. Precious lives.

"I saw Dr. Napier scowling in the gallery. I'm surprised you didn't have him in the OR with you, Dr. Chang," Mindy remarked as they scrubbed out. The neonatologists had whisked the babies off to the NICU in stable condition and Mindy had finished with Ms. Bayberry and she was in Recovery and stable as well.

Dr. Chang had stayed until the end, asking questions about the procedure.

Dr. Guild had always said it was a mark of a good surgeon to never stop learning and Mindy was a big believer in the Socratic method of teaching. Even if she was teaching a world-renowned and respected pediatric surgeon such as Dr. Amelia Chang.

"Professor Langley didn't want him in the OR, so I told him that there were too many people in the OR."

Mindy was confused. "Why would he not want Dr. Napier in the OR?"

Dr. Chang snorted. "Probably because Dr. Napier's mother complained to him about how many hours her son was getting in OB/GYN, seeing how she finds both our practices of medicine to be a waste of talent."

"Who is his mother?"

"Another surgeon. He doesn't like to say and I'm not in a position to divulge her name. Dr. Napier is pretty private."

"I get that. We all have secrets."

Dr. Chang cocked an eyebrow. "Yes."

"Does his mother have the same last name?"

"No, he has his father's name. His parents were married for a short while. I knew Dr. Napier's mother when she married Frasier Napier.

I really liked Dr. Napier's father, never cared for his mother too much."

"I don't blame you. She sounds like a real…"

"Pain?" Dr. Chang laughed. "Yeah, she is."

"I'm surprised that Dr. Napier never told me who his mother is."

"Now, that you'll have to ask Dr. Napier about. I doubt you'll get any answers from him, though. He's a private person. I don't even know why he keeps it to himself, but I respect his wishes." Dr. Chang finished scrubbing up and then left the scrub room, tossing her surgical cap in a receptacle on the way out.

Mindy finished her scrubbing and headed out too.

There were many more layers to Dr. Samuel Napier than met the eye. In the course of her career she'd met other physicians who'd had famous parents in the medical field and they had been quite proud to boast about that. Yet Sam didn't really talk about his mother much. He'd mentioned his father and family in Scotland with fondness, but nothing about his mother.

Don't pry.

She didn't want people to know about her humiliation in California.

That was her business and apparently Sam wanted to keep his secret about his mother private too and she respected that.

Besides, who was she to go prying? She was just an attending at the hospital he worked at and she was just someone he'd slept with once.

They weren't friends; they were no longer lovers. If he'd wanted to tell her about his mother, he would've.

Mindy scrubbed her hand over her face and headed toward her office, where she could dictate a report of the successful delivery of Ms. Bayberry's mono-amniotic twins while it was still fresh in her mind.

As she passed the skills lab, she could see someone hunched over a simulated womb, trying to insert a needle through to the fetus. Of course he was failing, because the sensors were going off and Sam was cursing in a very thick Scottish brogue.

Just leave him.

Only she couldn't. She was his teacher after all.

"Bloody hell."

"Is something wrong?" Mindy asked, as she shut the door to the skills lab behind her.

Sam glanced up. "Sorry, Dr. Walker. Did you need the skills lab?"

"No, no. I just happened to be walking by after Ms. Bayberry's surgery and saw you in here. Is everything okay? You didn't stay for the whole surgery."

"I'm fine. Once I saw the twins were going to make it, I left. My shift was over."

"Why didn't you go home?"

Sam shrugged. "It's lonely at home and I thought I would practice some other skills."

Mindy nodded and headed over to him. "Is there a particular reason you're cursing at this simulation?"

"Just a wee bit frustrated."

"Here, I can help." Mindy placed her hand over

his and then paused, removing her hand. "How about I show you?"

"Aye, that would be good." Sam handed her the catheter and needle and stood, moving out of the way so she had access to the simulation on the table.

Once again Mindy was very aware that Sam was standing very close to her. Why did she keep putting herself in the way of temptation?

Because you're weak.

"It requires a certain bit of skill to do this. The womb is strong but fragile, as is the life it holds inside. Are you watching?"

"Aye." Sam leaned in closer.

"Good." Mindy cleared her throat and then proceeded to show Sam how to do the procedure. "Keep your hands steady but firm. One wrong move…"

"I know. Can you do that again?" he asked.

"Of course." She removed the needle and reset the simulation. As she prepared to show him again, his hands slipped over hers, causing a zing of excitement to course through her as she recalled the way those strong hands had felt on her body, in her hair. "What're you doing?"

"I want to feel. Do you mind?"

Yes.

"No." Mindy's voice caught in her throat as the words came out. "Not at all."

His touch made her tremble slightly but she regained control of herself. The last thing she wanted to do was mess up the procedure or let Sam know how he affected her.

"Amazing," Sam whispered, his hot breath fanning her neck, causing gooseflesh to break out on her skin and down her back.

"It is. Do you want to try again?"

"Yes." He moved away from her and she got up. Sam took her place and she reset the simulation.

"You can do it." Mindy stood back and watched the monitors as Sam expertly copied the procedure. "See, I knew you could do it."

Sam nodded. "Thanks for your help, Mindy."

She frowned. "I don't think—"

"I know. You don't think I should be using

your first name, but in the last month you're the person I've talked to most and I believe I am your only friend in New York."

"We're friends?" Mindy asked.

Sam smiled, his blue eyes twinkling. "I'd like to think so. We can be friends, can't we? Co-workers can be friends. Just as long as you don't show me favoritism, we're okay."

Mindy chuckled. "Yeah, I think we can be friends, Dr. Napier."

"Sam."

"Sam." It felt right to say it again, but also wrong. She couldn't let him in. She was afraid.

"I'd just ask when we're on duty for you to call me Dr. Napier. The whole favoritism thing."

"That really bothers you."

"What does?" he asked.

"People thinking you're getting preferential treatment."

"Aye. It does."

"I know it does. Your accent thickens."

He grinned. "You are getting to know me well."

I tried not to. Only she didn't say that thought out loud.

"Well, that's what friends are for. Though I'm surprised you don't have many friends who are residents."

"I do, but they're not in my specialty and some have moved away."

"Oh, really? I never see them around."

Sam shrugged. "They're all busy with their own lives. I live with several of them in Brooklyn. I see them when I head back to my flat."

"I'm surprised you leave the hospital. I swear you live here."

"I could say the same for you, except I have seen your apartment." Then he frowned. "Sorry, Mindy. I didn't mean…"

Heat flushed her cheeks at the reminder that he'd been to her place. Slept in her bed…well, not exactly slept in her bed.

"I've been busy here. Consults, surgeries. I can't really set my own hours, like I did in my private practice."

Sam nodded. "When are you off next?"

"Tomorrow."

"Me too." Sam stood. "As a thank-you for helping me in the simulation lab I'd like to take you on a little tourist jaunt of New York City."

"A jaunt?" She asked. "Why?"

"You say that like I'm offering you a big bowl of the plague or something."

"I don't do jaunts," Mindy said.

"Oh, come on. Who doesn't do jaunts?"

"Me." Mindy chuckled.

"Well, you're going to go on one tomorrow," Sam said with finality.

"Fine. So where will this *jaunt* take us?"

"Have you seen all the touristy sights yet?"

"No. I haven't had time."

"Then it's settled. I'll pick you up tomorrow at nine a.m. sharp and we'll see all the sights of New York City."

"What? It's the middle of winter. It's cold out there."

Sam chuckled and headed toward the lab door. "I won't take no for an answer. You can dress in layers to fend off the cold, like any good New

Yorker would do. Besides, it's time to get you got acclimatized to the cold weather if you aim to remain in New York."

Mindy scowled. "What if I don't come downstairs at nine a.m.?"

"Then you'll leave me standing in the cold in front of your apartment, shouting your name."

Mindy gasped. "You wouldn't do that."

He cocked an eyebrow. "Oh, wouldn't I?"

"I wouldn't hear you high up in my penthouse."

"I don't care. I'll still do it."

"Fine," Mindy agreed grudgingly. "I'll dress in layers, but you'd better take me to all the really famous landmarks. Not the landmarks a native New Yorker *thinks* are famous. Like some weird house or building that was in some obscure movie in the eighties."

He laughed. "Agreed. I'll see you tomorrow, then."

Mindy's heart skipped a beat as he left the simulation lab, whistling something. What had she just done? This was not keeping her distance. This was the opposite.

She tried to tell herself that they were just friends. That this outing would be innocent. Nothing had to happen. Nothing needed to be said. They were just friends.

Yeah, keep telling yourself that.

CHAPTER SEVEN

I HOPE HE'S not down there, shouting.

Mindy was running late, though only by about five minutes. Still, she darted from the elevator and past the doorman out onto the street. She was terrified that Sam was going to make good on his promise and begin to shout her name.

When she rushed outside he was standing in front of her building, his hands deep in a black peacoat, looking up toward the sky. Then he looked at her and grinned, that cocky, devilish smile that made her weak in the knees.

"I thought you'd be out here, screaming my name," Mindy said as she walked over to him.

"Well, I was contemplating it but I remembered that your place is a penthouse and that's a bloody tall building."

Mindy chuckled. "It's the best."

He cocked an eyebrow. "You really think so? I prefer the brownstone myself. That's why I live in one."

"I thought you lived in an apartment with a bunch of other residents?"

"Aye, but the flats are in a brownstone. It's kind of just a bedroom really. Though one of my roommates moved in with her boyfriend recently."

"You live with girls. Why does that not surprise me?" she teased.

"There is one other man in the house."

"Sure, sure."

"There is. I don't know why you don't believe me. What have I got to hide?"

"A harem."

Sam snorted. "Oh, aye, a harem of surgical residents."

Mindy rolled her eyes and then laughed. "So, what do you have planned for us today since you were so insistent that I spend my day off touring New York City in the freezing cold temperatures."

"This *isn't* cold."

"It is when you're from California."

"Aye, well. Yes, I guess so."

"How do the Scots keep warm? Especially when wearing kilts?"

Sam groaned. "I'm not wearing a kilt. Why are you bringing up kilts now?"

"Because you're making fun of the fact that I'm from California and I hate the cold."

"I had porridge this morning."

Mindy wrinkled his nose. "Ugh."

"It keeps you warm. It's hearty."

"No, thanks," Mindy said.

"You need to toughen up, Mindy." Then he slipped his arm through hers. "And we'll start by dragging you out on a ferry to visit one of my favorite ladies."

"You told me that we were going to see traditional tourist attractions. I don't want to visit one of your girlfriends on some obscure island."

He looked at her like she was crazy. "I was talking about the Statue of Liberty, you daft hen."

She glared at him.

"What's that look for?" he asked.

"For calling me a daft hen!"

"I'm sorry."

"Oh, well, that's okay."

Sam chuckled as they walked toward the subway station. "You were a wee bit jealous when you thought I was going to drag you to meet a girlfriend."

"Hardly."

"Aye, you were." His eyes were twinkling. "Admit it."

"I'm not going to admit to anything and you can't make me. So how are we going to get to the Statue of Liberty?" she asked, changing the subject of jealously and girlfriends, because he was right, the thought of him with another woman drove her a bit bonkers. It made her see green, though it shouldn't. She didn't have a claim on him.

"We're going to take the Number One train down to the South Ferry Station."

Mindy dug in her heels. "We're taking the subway?"

"What're you worrying about? There's nothing wrong with taking the subway."

"I've never taken public transportation before."

"Never?"

She shook her head. "In Los Angeles it wasn't safe."

"Well, it would take you all day in this kind of traffic to get down to the South Ferry Station and even then it would be almost impossible and probably expensive to find parking. I also don't have a car. Do you?"

"No. I've been meaning to go and look…"

Sam *tsked* under his breath. "Trust me. Don't waste your money. If you want to leave the city for some reason, rent a car. Trust me, the subway train will not bite you."

He took her gloved hand and squeezed it. "Do you trust me?" he asked.

"I have no choice."

Sam laughed. "Aye, that's true. Come on. I swear it will be fun."

Mindy let him lead her down the steps of the Eighty-Sixth Street Station into the underground of New York City. The first thing she noticed was that it was warm but the air was dank and smelled stale. She wrinkled her nose but followed him through the turnstiles as he paid their fare and he led her to the platform.

She gripped his arm, holding on to him for dear life, and he teased her.

"Do you think I'm going to push you off to meet your maker?"

"If you do, I'm taking you with me," she said.

He laughed again. She liked the way he laughed, it always made her smile.

"Deal," he said. "But I promise you I won't be throwing you over the edge. It would be a waste of a beautiful woman."

Heat bloomed in Mindy's cheeks. She wanted to chastise him for saying that, but they were alone. They weren't on duty. They were just two friends exploring the city and she didn't have a problem with him telling her she was beautiful.

There was a rumbling sound and she peeked down the dark tunnel to see two headlights in the distance.

"Come on, we have to move to the front of the train and get one of the first five compartments."

"Why?" Mindy asked, as Sam guided her down to the other end of the platform.

"They only allow the first five compartments of the train to exit at the South Ferry Station. I don't know why, but that's just the way it is."

The train slowed and stopped, the breeze blowing her loose hair into her face as it pulled into the station. The doors opened and a few people got off. Once the way was clear Sam pushed his way on, dragging her with him.

Surprisingly, there was a seat and he sat her down and stood in front of her. The doors dinged shut and the train pulled out of the station and down the dark tunnel.

"I feel bad with you standing there."

"Don't feel bad. I don't think you should be standing on your first ride on the subway. Maybe

when we head back up to the Upper West Side."
He winked at her, holding tight to the handhold
above him, his body swaying back and forth
with the train.

They chatted the best they could during their
subway ride to the South Street Ferry. It was
hard, with the constant jolting coupled with the
loading and unloading of people.

"Come on. Up you get." He held out his free
hand and helped her to her feet.

"Why?" she asked, as she held on for dear life.

"The next stop is ours and we have to get off
as quickly as we can before people start pushing to get on."

Sam gripped her hand tight as the train came to
a stop and the doors opened. He led her through
the throng of people and out onto the platform.
He guided her through the crowd and up to street
level, where they headed to the Battery to catch
the ferry to take them to Liberty Park.

Mindy shivered in the cold wind. "Do they
operate on bitter days like today?"

"The only day they don't run is December twenty-fifth and this is not bitter, you big wimp."

She punched him in the arm but didn't let go of his hand as they walked to the ferries. As they approached the depot she could see signs about pre-booking to enter the pedestal and the crown of the Statue of Liberty.

"You have to reserve your tickets in advance."

"Don't worry. I booked them last night. Got the last two tickets for this morning." He glanced at her briefly as they waited in line. "You're trying to figure out a way out of this. Why?"

"Why? Because it's freaking cold. What if the boat sinks and we're eaten by sharks?"

Sam cocked an eyebrow. "Are you afraid of the water?"

"I'm not afraid of water. I'm afraid of sharks and drowning. Oh, and hypothermia."

He laughed. "You're a strange duck, Mindy Walker."

"I'm going to take that as a compliment."

"As you should." Sam winked and they boarded

the ferry, which would take them on a short ride out on said frigid waters toward Lady Liberty, who faced southeast, greeting all newcomers to the U.S.A. Even though it was cold outside, it was sunny. A brilliant sunny day that reflected off the patina of the statue and her torch, making her seem to glow. Mindy had seen so many pictures of her but hadn't really paid attention to this famous landmark when she'd arrived in New York just over a month ago. Now close up to her she could see why people loved her. Mindy leaned over the rail, smiling.

"When you smile like that, you're really quite stunning," Sam said.

"You really shouldn't flatter me like that."

"Why?" he asked.

"I might let it go to my head and forget myself." Then she blushed, the heat rushing to her cheeks, even though it was cold. Why was she flirting with him? He was off-limits. Only she couldn't help herself. It was easy around him.

Too easy.

Sam's eyes twinkled, but he didn't respond.

Instead, he leaned over the railing beside her and though she was kind of hoping he would say something, she was glad that he didn't. She hadn't meant to say what she had, but she really had forgotten herself for a moment and who she was with. It was nice.

It had been so long since she'd been at ease around a man.

She'd forgotten how good it felt to have that kind of intimacy with someone and she really missed it.

Sam was surprised by what she'd said.

"I might let it go to my head and forget myself."

He'd momentarily forgotten who he was with, but when she'd said those words his blood had heated with desire. Mindy looked so delectable all bundled up. Her soft purple knitted hat and infinity scarf set off the color of her eyes against her dark, rich red hair and he fought the desire to pull her up against him and kiss her, because at this moment all he could remember was the taste of her lips.

They had been so sweet.

All he could think about was her body naked with his. His lips on her ivory throat, his hands in her silky hair.

Get a grip on yourself, man.

So he didn't say anything in response to her, just leaned over the railing and tried to focus on their approach to Liberty Island. He was hoping the cold wind biting at his cheeks would take away the lust singing in his blood.

He couldn't remember the last time he'd wanted a woman like this. Other than the first night they'd met, but even then if she hadn't initiated the kiss, if she hadn't asked him back to her apartment, he probably would've done nothing.

Vixen that she was, he was absolutely lost to her and he knew he was so weak that if she asked him now to take her in his arms, he would without hesitation.

She's off-limits.

And he had to keep reminding himself of that fact.

They were friends and nothing more. He wouldn't walk down the same path his mother had. He wouldn't sleep or have a relationship with a doctor who was his attending before he was. If she was still available when his fellowship was over, and he was an attending in his own right, then perhaps they could revisit their night of passion.

But, really, who was he kidding? He still had a couple years of working in the pediatric field before he became an attending. By then she would have moved on. A beautiful, funny, compassionate and talented surgeon like Mindy would have no problem finding someone. If only she would open up.

There were a few walls she'd carefully constructed around her.

It's why he had a feeling she didn't have many friends and he couldn't figure out why she was keeping people out of her life. Why she was so closed off.

Any time they had come close to talking about something personal her walls had gone up. Of course, the same applied to him. His personal life was just that. Personal, and very few people knew his secrets. He preferred it that way. Fewer rumors that way.

"You hear about Dr. Hanley? The only reason she got that spot was because she slept with her attending, Dr. Langley."

"Yes, and it totally destroyed her marriage. I feel bad. She has a son. Poor kid."

The problem was the "poor kid" had been him, and he'd heard every word those other surgeons had said about his mother. It still stung to this day and he refused to be lumped in with his mother, even though he seriously doubted Mindy was as much of a jerk as the professor was. If it hadn't been for the fact that Dr. Chang was at West Manhattan Saints he would never have applied to the surgical program.

He avoided Langley as much as he could, because he was one of the reasons his parents had split up. Why his mother had a reputation that followed her brilliance. Why people admired her, lauded her, but talked behind her back.

Sam didn't want that.

"Thank goodness!" Mindy exclaimed, breaking through his morose thoughts. "We're finally going to be on dry land."

Sam chuckled. "There, now the sharks can't get you. Unless I push you off the island."

Mindy turned toward him. "You do that and, like at the subway station, I'm going to take you with me. You're bigger, they'll eat you first."

Sam grinned but didn't respond as he took her outstretched arm and they headed down to the lower deck to get off the boat and check out the Statue of Liberty.

He tried to keep his mind off the fact he was with one of the most beautiful women he'd seen for a long time and instead focus on the interesting museum in the pedestal of the Statue of Liberty.

Okay, the museum was not that interesting and he'd been to it before, but Mindy seemed engrossed in looking over everything.

"You're absolutely and utterly bored, aren't you?" Mindy asked, peering over a display, not looking at him.

"How can you possibly know that? You're not paying attention to me at all."

She smiled to herself. "I know when someone is bored. You've been shifting your weight on the balls of your feet, whistling and just trailing behind me."

"Okay, the museum isn't my cup of tea. I've been here before."

"I figured as much," she said. "I do appreciate you bringing me."

"Not a problem."

"Should we race to the top?" she teased.

"Are you kidding? It's like over two hundred stairs to the top."

"It's three hundred and fifty-four, to be precise, but of course you would've known that had you read what I just read." And for good measure she made a superior face.

"Why, you little…"

Mindy laughed and raced to the stairwell,

taking the stairs quickly while Sam chased her. They didn't run the whole way, they took breaks and stopped their mad chase when they came across others who were tackling the spiral staircase at a more leisurely pace and probably thought they were out of their gourds, racing around a national monument.

When they got to the top Sam leaned against the wall to catch his breath for a moment, so he didn't sound too winded in front of her.

"You're such an old man," Mindy teased.

"I'm younger than you."

"Low blow, old man Napier. Very low blow indeed."

Sam grinned and came up beside her so they could look out over the water. Even though it was chilly out, the brilliant morning sun reflected against the water like diamonds.

"It is beautiful," Mindy admitted. "I'm glad you brought me out here to see this. Even if it's cold."

"You're welcome." He glanced at her, actually he couldn't take his eyes off of her, watching her delight in their trip. "Well, we'd better head down if we're going to get to our next destination in time."

Mindy cocked an eyebrow. "Next destination. No, we don't need to go anywhere else. This was great."

"I won't hear any arguments. We're going to the Empire State Building."

"What is with your obsession with tall buildings today?"

"I'm taking you to all the touristy spots, like I said I would. I can't help it that a lot of touristy spots are tall buildings. Well, two are for sure." And he winked at her. "You're at my mercy today, Mindy."

Mindy just rolled her eyes and then laughed. "Whatever you say."

Sam chuckled as he followed her down the endless steps back to the pedestal of the Statue of Liberty. He kept his hands firmly jammed in his pockets so as not to reach out and pull her into his arms.

The idea of having her at his mercy excited him.

Stop thinking that way or you'll be in trouble.

It seemed to him that he had to keep reminding himself of this fact.

Frequently.

It was hard not to, though. There were so many things he liked about Mindy. Even though she seemed to have her own walls firmly in place, keeping him out, she still was this bright, shiny and happy person. Her brilliance, her enthusiasm for everything she put herself into appealed to him.

She had fire in her. When residents or interns displeased her, especially when working on a fragile case, when a mother and her unborn baby's lives were at stake, she was a fierce protector of her patients.

Dr. Mindy Walker was someone you didn't want to cross professionally, but sometimes he got the feeling that she wasn't always like that. That the fierceness was a defense mechanism, part of the walls.

He'd done a bit of research about her, read some of her papers. She'd had a very lucrative practice in California. What would make her sell it, pack up her life and move to a place where the air hurt her face?

Sam chuckled again to himself as he thought of her saying that a couple times since they'd left her apartment.

"Why am I living where the air hurts my face?"

And then she would make a pouty face.

"Ugh," she groaned, as they stepped outside and headed toward the dock to pick up their ferry back to Battery Park.

"Yeah, yeah, the air. It hurts."

Mindy punched him in the arm. "Smart aleck."

They boarded the ferry and soon they were pushing off away from the Statue of Liberty. This time they sat on the benches inside. He leaned back against the bench, his arms spread, and she leaned back into his arm. She didn't snuggle in but she didn't move away either.

It was nice.

"So, why did you move here again?"

Mindy cleared her throat. "I told you. It was an

opportunity I couldn't pass up. Professor Langley made me an offer I couldn't refuse."

Sam snorted at the mention of the chief of surgery. "I see."

"You don't really like Professor Langley, do you?"

"What do you mean?" Sam straightened up and crossed his arms.

"Aha, so you have some secrets too."

Sam shrugged. "We just don't get on, that's all."

"That's funny, because I could've sworn that he mentioned to me that you were one of the residents to watch."

The compliment just slid off of him. He didn't care if Langley thought highly of him. If it had been Dr. Chang that would've been different. He respected Dr. Chang. In fact, he respected most of the surgeons as West Manhattan Saints except Langley, because he'd ruined his parents' marriage.

"Was it worth it, Monica? The promotion

meant so much to you, you felt it necessary to throw our marriage away?"

"You don't understand me, Frasier. You don't understand what it's like being a surgeon. Being the best. Langley understands my needs. You don't. You just want me to be a mother, a house-wife, grubbing around on your land in the High-lands. That's not what I want. That's not what I deserve. I never wanted to be a mother!"

His parents' last fight haunted him.

The heartbreak in his father's voice because his father had truly loved his mother. Sam's father had been blinded by love to the point that he had fallen in love with someone who didn't value love and family the same way he did.

It had nearly destroyed his father and it cut Sam to the quick when she hadn't wanted full custody of him. That he'd moved from New York to Scotland. In the end, living with his father and being raised in the Highlands had given him a happy childhood, but it was the rejection of the woman he called Mother that still hurt.

When he had visited her, she'd barely spent any time with him unless he'd been in the hospital with her and he'd got to watch her and Langley together.

It was when she'd taken her posting at Harvard and left West Manhattan Saints that he'd stopped visiting her as often, because she hadn't had time for him.

"What's wrong?" Mindy asked. "You just totally closed off."

"Just thinking." Sam gave her a half-smile. "We're here. You ready for your next adventure?"

"And if I say no?"

"You don't have a choice, remember? I'm in charge today." He held his hand out and she took it as they disembarked from the ferry and moved through the crowds heading to the subway station so they could catch the next ride up to the Empire State Building.

Sam shook the thoughts of his mother from his head.

His mother was not allowed in today. She

wasn't going to ruin this day. This day was all about him and Mindy.

Today he was going to have fun too, because he couldn't remember the last time he'd had this much fun.

CHAPTER EIGHT

MINDY PEERED THROUGH the binoculars on the top of the Empire State Building. Usually she wasn't one for heights—she wasn't afraid of them, but she didn't go out of her way to visit tall buildings and ride an elevator to the top of one.

At least the Statue of Liberty had stairs, but the Empire State Building had an elevator and she didn't really like elevators or their enclosed spaces too much, but she just squeezed Sam's hand tight.

He gave her an encouraging smile and squeezed her hand back, but once they were at the top it was fine and she was glad she was able to have a nice vantage point of the city. It was truly beautiful.

She could only imagine what it would be like

to be at the top of the Empire State Building as the sun was setting. From her penthouse apartment, when she actually looked out her window at night, she would stare at this building all lit up. Another true icon of the city she was slowly growing to love.

And she was.

She may not be used to the winters yet, but she could see the appeal of living and *making* it in New York.

Sam shivered beside her.

"Now who's cold?" she teased, as she focused the viewfinder on him. The money had run out so she couldn't see anything anymore, but he didn't know that.

He tutted under his breath. "Well, it's a bit windy up here. At least when we were at the top of the Statue of Liberty we were in an enclosed space. This is out in the open."

"Okay, well, how about we head down? I'm a bit hungry. Do you want to grab a slice of pizza? Isn't that the traditional thing to do in New York City?"

"We're not going for a slice."

"We're not?" She was a bit disappointed.

"No, I have somewhere better we can go."

"But you're not going to tell me, are you?"

He shook his head and grinned in that annoying but sexy way of his.

"Did anyone mention that you're a pain, Dr. Napier?"

"Aye, several times. Especially my roommates. Remember, most of them are female."

"Right. You did mention that. Oh, didn't I see one of your former roommates on the OB/GYN list for an appointment? Uh, Dr. Camara?"

Sam frowned. "Yes, she's pregnant, but she's seeing you? Is something wrong?" There was genuine concern in his voice.

"No, nothing is wrong. I happened to be a licensed OB/GYN as well. I was covering for another doctor. There's nothing wrong there." She smiled. "It's nice, you know?"

"What is?" he asked, as they stood in line, waiting for the elevator to go down.

"That you care about your friends so much, but I don't think you show it much."

Sam snorted. "Of course I care. She's pregnant. I wouldn't want anything to happen to her or the baby."

"Okay, now you're putting the accent on thick, and as you're not annoyed you're doing it on purpose."

"Does that bother you?" he asked, a twinkle of devilment in his eyes.

Yes. It turns me on.

And Mindy could distinctly remember the last time his thick accent had turned her on. She'd jumped into his arms when he'd been a perfect stranger and had begged him to go home with her. When they'd been at her apartment his brogue had been thick the more aroused he'd become, and just thinking about it made her hot under the collar.

"No, it doesn't bother me in the least."

Liar.

"Then why even bring it up?" Sam teased.

"If you don't shut it soon I'm going to…"

Sam leaned over to whisper in her ear. "You're going to what, Dr. Walker?"

Mindy was going to retaliate but the doors to the elevator opened and they shuffled on and were surrounded by other people. So she kept her mouth shut, but she could see Sam smirking to himself, because he knew she wouldn't continue the conversation on an elevator crammed full of people.

He was such a pain in the butt.

At least it was a fast ride down. Once they were out on the street and the crowd of people leaving the lobby of the Empire State Building dispersed she turned to him.

"What now?"

"Now I'm going to take you for lunch," he said with a wink.

"How do I even know I'm going to like this lunch? I mean, you won't tell me where we're going," Mindy groused.

"You'll like it. Well, maybe you won't. I don't know what kind of food you like. Perhaps I should've asked you that before I made reservations."

"I like pizza."

Sam winced. "Sorry, no pizza where we're going."

"Am I dressed okay, then? You said you made reservations." She was dressed casually. She wasn't dressed in her yoga attire, but still it wasn't business casual. "Will jeans and a nice sweater do for wherever it is you're taking me?"

He stood back and rubbed his chin while she spun around. "Well, I don't know. I guess you'll do."

Mindy punched him playfully in the arm. "I'm *so* putting you on scut duty for a month."

He laughed out loud and grabbed her mittened hand. "You can't do that, Dr. Walker. I'm not on your service."

"Oh, I can. I can have a few choice words with Dr. Chang…"

"Blackmail. I see."

They both laughed and Mindy let Sam lead her wherever he was planning on taking her. Not that she was too impressed they were walking but, then, she found the wind wasn't biting as much anymore.

Maybe she was really getting acclimatized, which was a scary thought. She'd never thought she would ever get used to winter.

"You're frowning," Sam remarked.

"The cold isn't bothering me."

He chuckled. "I knew you'd get used to it."

"Well, just because I'm used to it doesn't mean I like it. Why couldn't we have taken a cab?"

"It's not that far away." Sam pointed. "See, it's just across the street."

Mindy looked to where he was pointing and saw the red canopied entranceway to The Russian Tea Room.

"Oh!"

"I take it that meets your approval?" Sam asked.

"It does."

"Come on or we'll be late for our reservations."

They dashed across West Fifty-Seventh Street, dodging cars and taxi cabs. The door was opened for them by the doorman, who doffed his hat as they entered the exquisite entrance of the world-famous Russian Tea Room.

"Wow," Mindy whispered, as she pulled off her knitted hat. She'd seen pictures of it, heard about it and knew it was featured in several famous television shows, but standing in the lushly red decorated Russian Tea Room in person, well, she realized pictures and television didn't do it justice. The dark green walls, with gold imperial eagles emblazoned on them, gave the room a vibe of decadence and mystery.

Sam spoke to the host and they were escorted to a corner booth, which was offset and away from some other afternoon diners. They settled into the booth.

"I thought it would be busier," Mindy said, shrugging out of her jacket.

"We missed the lunch crowd, it's time for early tea."

"Tea?"

"Well, I do come from Scotland. We do have

tea and I frankly haven't had a proper tea in a long time."

Mindy leaned on her elbow. "You know, the more you use the word 'tea,' the more it loses its meaning."

"Tea, tea, tea." Sam opened the menu. "How adventurous are you when it comes to cuisine? I mean, you did tell me your favorite food was pizza."

"I think I'm pretty adventurous, but I draw the line at blood sausage. I know exactly what that is and I'm not interested."

"Oh, come on, it's not that...you're right, but it sounds worse than it is. Black pudding is more English than Russian, though."

"So what do you want me to try?"

"How about caviar?" Sam asked. "It's been a while since I had some."

"Are you serious?"

"Very." He cocked his head to one side. "Does the idea of caviar gross you out?"

"No it doesn't gross me out. I'm willing to try anything. Once."

Sam grinned and when the waiter came he ordered a royal afternoon tea for two. When Mindy glanced at the menu she had no idea where she was going to put all that food. She was hungry, but blinis, assorted sandwiches and caviar sounded a little rich.

As she watched Sam conversing in a friendly way with the waiter, she smiled. She couldn't help herself. When she and Dean had gone out to dinner, he had treated the wait staff, or anyone in the service industry, with disdain, like they were beneath him, no better than the dirt under his shoe. It had got to the stage that Mindy hadn't actually liked going out with Dean half the time. Even after the awkward relationship with their waiter there hadn't been much to talk about. They'd just eaten, possibly talked about cases.

There had been no spark.

She was spending the day with Sam and not once had she thought about when it would end. It was easy being with him. So easy.

Too easy.

No, she'd sworn now was the time she was going to focus on herself. She was going to find herself again.

They could only be friends. Nothing more.

It was a nice thought to entertain, because that's all it could be. Just a fantasy.

Sam was totally relaxed for the first time in… well, he couldn't remember when. Mindy, when she wasn't Dr. Walker, was a vivacious and funny woman to be around. The more time he spent with her the more he wanted to be with her.

"You're lonely. You need to find someone."

Kimberlyn's words seemed to strike a chord with him once again. Maybe she was right after all. Settling down, having someone had never been on his radar. At least, not until after he had his career set, but even then he wasn't sure if he could give his all to his career and a family.

He hadn't had the best role model when it came to surgeons and families.

Then again, he knew colleagues who made it work.

All he had to do was start by looking at his roommates. Especially Enzo and Kimberlyn. A relationship that had started with them being competitors. Then they'd both turned down a fellowship with Dr. Ootaka in favor of the other getting it. Now, that was love. And those two were joined at the hip.

Maybe I can have it all?

He shook that thought out of his head as fast as he could.

No. He couldn't have it all. At least, not with Mindy. It was bad enough that his mother's reputation could ruin him if people found out he was her son, but to start up a relationship with an attending when that surgeon was responsible for deciding if he got a fellowship or not could not happen.

He would not have that haunting his career.

The waiter brought their tea and set down two glass tea cups that had ornate pewter handles and delicate pewter carving wrapped all around them.

"Oh! So pretty," Mindy gushed, and then set the cup down to let the waiter pour her tea.

Sam couldn't help but smile as he watched her. *Dammit. Why her?*

Why had she had to walk into that bar that night? Why had he gone with her back up to her apartment? Why did he have to want the one woman he couldn't have?

"You never do things the easy way, son. You always take the hardest road to hoe."

Sam took a sip of his tea, mulling over his father's words. It was true. Nothing ever came very easily for him. He had to work hard for things, but it made him appreciate it all the more when he achieved his goal.

Sure, he could've done his fellowship at his mother's hospital. He could've had his surgical training handed to him on a silver platter. Lord knew, he knew enough children of physicians who did just that, but he hadn't wanted his training to be handed to him.

And he most definitely didn't want to work with his mother or be under her thumb.

"This is really great," Mindy said with a contented sigh. "It almost makes me not want to go into work tomorrow. Almost."

"Really? I didn't think tea would have that effect on you."

"I have a busy caseload tomorrow. I have a mother being transported in from upstate. She's pregnant with quintuplets."

Sam raised his eyebrows. "Quints? Do you need a resident tomorrow?"

"I thought you had tomorrow off as well?" Mindy teased.

"I can also switch a shift. How often do you come across quints?"

"In my line of work, often enough." Mindy leaned back against the booth. "Those mono-amniotic twins, however, those are rare."

"I'd like to assist if I may."

Mindy grinned at him. "When the time comes. I am trying to keep those babies inside her for a bit longer. I don't want them to be born too premature."

"So the quints are the only thing on your docket tomorrow?" he asked.

"No, not the only thing. I have a few client consultations. I'm considered one of the top infertility doctors in the country, so it keeps me pretty busy."

"You're a surgeon of many talents."

"I should hope so. I spent enough time in my fellowships." She looked a little wistful. "Missed out a bit on things."

"Aye, but it must've been worth it."

"Oh, yes, it was. I wouldn't change my education for anything."

Sam leaned across the table. "You studied at Stanford?"

Mindy nodded. "Like I said before, I'm a native Californian. Never really traveled much. I liked the west coast too much."

"Which begs the question again, why did you leave?" He knew he'd touched a part that was hidden behind one of her walls. The sparkle in her eye disappeared and her spine stiffened. She wouldn't look him in the eye either, just traced her long, delicate fingers over the filigree on her cup.

"I told you, the chief made me an offer I couldn't refuse."

Sam knew better than to press the subject. He didn't want this day to end on a sour note. If he couldn't have her the way he wanted her, he wanted them to remain friends. He wanted to continue to work with her, learn from her because she was a brilliant surgeon.

"Right. I forgot."

The waiter brought a tray of assorted sandwiches and blinis with caviar. Sam thanked the waiter and then held out a blini with caviar on it.

"So, you said you were how adventurous when it comes to your food?"

The smile returned to Mindy's face. "No way out of this, is there?"

"Nope."

She held out her plate and he gave her one. The rest of the tea went well. They talked about the hospital, about cases, about New York, and neither of them pried further into the other's personal life.

It was a nice, friendly tea.

When it was over he hailed a cab and they took a taxi back to her apartment. He walked her to the door and stood under the canopy with her, not wanting their day to end but knowing that it must.

"I had a great time today, Sam. Thank you for showing this California girl around New York."

"It was no problem. I'd been meaning to revisit some of those spots myself. I hadn't been to the Statue of Liberty since I was a young boy."

"Well, I'm glad you took me."

"Me too."

An awkward silence fell between them. They just stood there. He wanted to reach out, run his hands over her cheek and pull her into a kiss. That's usually how he ended dates when he was dating.

Only he couldn't with her.

"I'll see you in the morning, Sam." Mindy turned and disappeared inside.

Sam sighed, jammed his hands into his pockets and left to catch the subway back to his lonely flat in Brooklyn.

Not that he'd be alone as most of his roommates were off tonight, but without Mindy the world seemed like a pretty hollow, lonely and empty place.

It was the same world he woke up in every day, but after spending one day with Mindy he realized just how lonely he was.

CHAPTER NINE

MINDY TRIED NOT to let her gaze wander to Sam as she walked into the boardroom. It had been a week since their day in New York together. When he'd walked her to the door of her apartment she'd lingered.

She didn't know why. Perhaps it had been habit. She had been waiting for him to kiss her, even though kissing him again wouldn't have been wise.

Yet she'd waited there and he hadn't done anything. Just stood with her, his blue eyes dark, his face unreadable.

She actually didn't know why he'd waited there either, but the more he'd lingered the more she'd fought herself over inviting him up to her apartment. Of course, the last time she'd done that they'd slept together and she couldn't do that again.

Though she'd wanted to.

Being with Sam was so easy. She admired and respected him as a surgeon; he was fun, sexy, intelligent. Sexy.

Stop thinking about sex and his sexiness.

Only she couldn't when she was around him. *Focus.*

Right now she had in front of her a skilled team of pediatricians, neonatologists, nurse practitioners, residents, anesthesiologists, just about anyone who could possibly help with her quint case. Mindy had been keeping an eye on Mrs. Jameson for about a week, but it was apparent to Mindy that with Mrs. Jameson's condition they would have to prepare an elite team of practitioners in preparation for the quints' birth.

It was coming sooner rather than later.

She glanced up quickly to see that Sam was sitting next to Dr. Chang, leaning back in the chair, focused on her intently. When their gazes met he smiled, just briefly.

It sent a zing through her.

Before she could get started, though, there was a knock and Professor Langley stepped into the room.

"My apologies, Dr. Walker. I hope I haven't missed anything."

"No, of course not. Come in."

He nodded and then waved to someone else who was standing just outside the door. "I hope you don't mind, but I read the case file on the quints. I noticed one of them had a brain bleed that might need to be addressed."

"Yes. I was about to talk about the medical conditions of the babies."

"I thought you might want the help of one of the finest neurosurgeons. So I brought in Dr. Hanley." He stepped aside and Dr. Hanley stepped into the room.

Mindy's eyes widened. There was a collective gasp. Everyone knew who Dr. Hanley was. Who didn't? She was one of the most renowned and respected neurosurgeons.

"Thank you for allowing me to join you." Dr. Hanley's gaze fell on Dr. Chang and Sam. "Dr. Chang."

There was an odd tone to Dr. Hanley's greeting and as Mindy glanced at Sam she could see he was not happy. His lips were pressed together in a firm line of annoyance.

Mindy knew he had issues with Professor Langley, but open hostility wouldn't be good for his career and could impede his fellowship.

"You can proceed now, Dr. Walker," Professor Langley, the chief of surgery, said, taking a seat next to Dr. Hanley.

"Thank you." Mindy turned to the computer and brought up an ultrasound and Mrs. Jameson's medical records. "As you can see, Mrs. Jameson is a thirty-four-year-old female whose LMP was approximately thirty weeks ago today. She is Gravida One and Parity X. That pregnancy resulted in a forty-week-term delivery of a healthy baby boy who weighed approximately eight pounds seven ounces. There were no complications."

Mindy went on with her presentation, explaining about the different quints, and began to set out the teams that would be responsible for each baby. Most of the babies didn't seem to have a whole lot of medical problems. The fact that Mrs. Jameson had gotten to thirty weeks was a blessing, but she was starting to have frequent contractions and Mindy knew she had to get the teams prepared now, because once one of the waters broke that was it. It was time to get those babies out.

"As you can see, it's baby C that has fluid buildup around his brain and baby C is the one we're most concerned with." Mindy clicked on a close-up of baby C.

Dr. Hanley got up and walked over to the screen. "Hmm, I would need some more comprehensive films, but it looks like a simple shunt would take care of that. We should closely monitor that buildup of fluid, Dr. Walker. If it continues, we shouldn't delay in delivering the babies."

"I agree, Dr. Hanley," Mindy said. "I'll have that set up for you right away."

"Do." Dr. Hanley didn't even really acknowledge her as she headed back to her seat beside Professor Langley.

She'd heard rumors that Dr. Hanley was a piece of work. She could see why. Unfazed, Mindy went on with her presentation and went on to assign the teams that were responsible for each baby.

As she was about to assign Sam to Dr. Chang's team, Dr. Hanley stood up.

"If you don't mind, Dr. Walker, I would request that Dr. Napier be on my team for Baby C. I would like him to work on the shunt with me."

Sam's eyes narrowed and he scowled, not at all impressed.

"I think Dr. Chang requires Dr. Napier's assistance," Mindy said, and then regretted it. She didn't want anyone to think she was playing favorites.

Dr. Hanley glared at her now. "Nonsense, he's a resident and I require his assistance."

"Dr. Napier can work with Dr. Hanley," the chief of surgery said, standing up. "I trust there were will be no further discussions. Keep us updated on the patient, Dr. Walker."

He excused himself and Dr. Hanley followed him.

Mindy was absolutely confused. She knew that Dr. Hanley was a brilliant surgeon but so was she. Yet they were bending over backwards to accommodate Dr. Hanley.

As people began to disperse Dr. Chang leaned over to a visibly angry Sam and whispered a few words, but he rebuffed her, stood and stormed out of the room.

What in the world?

She knew Sam didn't like orders from Chief Langley and didn't like time taken from pediatrics, but he was having a shot at working with Dr. Hanley. He shouldn't look a gift horse in the mouth.

Dr. Chang sent her a furtive glance but didn't say anything else. She just left the room quietly. Mindy couldn't help but wonder what was up be-

tween Dr. Hanley, the chief and Sam. Any time
Professor Langley was mentioned Sam would
tense up.

What did he have against him?

Curiosity killed the cat.

Even though she really wanted to know what
was going on, she knew it wasn't her business.
She wasn't going to pry or push. When Sam was
ready to tell her, he'd tell her, though she was really dying to know. Besides, she didn't exactly
open up to him and she wouldn't. There had to
be a good reason Sam kept it secret and she'd
respect his wishes. Some things could destroy
a career very fast.

Mindy sighed and cleaned up her presentation. She shouldn't be fussing over why Sam
was upset. The teams had been set up. Her focus
should be on her patient. On those babies. That's
why she'd come to West Manhattan Saints. She'd
come to provide the best medical care, to focus
on her career.

Let Dr. Chang, the chief and Dr. Hanley deal
with fighting over Sam.

She couldn't worry about it.

Sam had to deal with his own problems.

Sam was furious. What the heck was his mother doing here? He was also so angry that she'd called him out like that, requesting him and taking him off Dr. Chang's service. He was sure the surgery his mother wanted him to work on, placing a shunt on Baby C, would be exciting, but he'd rather learn the procedure from anyone but his mother.

Not that he'd have an actual chance to participate in the surgery. His mother didn't really involve her residents. She didn't let them get their hands dirty. Sam knew his mother well. She liked to hog all the glory.

His mother was speaking to Langley at the end of the hallway. She was touching his arm and laughing in an intimate way. It made Sam's teeth grind, seeing them together, because it instantly brought back the memory of his father holding his hand almost twenty years ago and the look of heartache on his father's face as he'd realized his wife was cheating on him.

They finished talking and Langley walked away. His mother turned around and smiled, briefly. Not in a warm compassionate way, or in a way that showed she was glad to see him. It was polite.

"Well, I can tell by your expression you're not exactly happy to see me, Dr. Napier."

Sam was pleased that at least he was keeping his anonymity.

"Perhaps we should take this somewhere more private."

His mother smirked. "Of course. My temporary office is down the hall."

Sam nodded and followed behind his mother as she led him to the office she was using. His stomach knotted when he saw all the boxes. How long was temporary?

She shut the door and Sam crossed his arms.

"I know that look," his mother said. "You're not happy that I'm here."

"Aye."

She chuckled. "So like your father."

"What are you doing here?" Sam asked, not wanting her to talk about his father with him. She had no right.

"That's the way you talk to your mother after not seeing her for five years?"

"I didn't think you cared particularly."

She shrugged and then tossed her blonde hair over her shoulder. "I kept busy."

So like his mother. She didn't admit to caring. It infuriated him.

"What're you doing here, Mother?"

"Saving a life?"

Sam glanced around at the boxes. "Dr. Walker requested your presence? I thought she only just discovered the issue with Baby C in the last week."

"No Dr. Walker did not request my presence. Gareth did."

Sam cringed inwardly at his mother's familiarity with Langley. It was another kick in the pants to him. A reminder about how she and Langley had broken his family apart.

"Again. Why?"

"There's a patient here in your pediatric ward. One with an inoperable brain tumor."

"Janie?" Sam asked.

His mother nodded. "Her parents have agreed to allow me to try and resect it using a new technique. That's why I'm here for some time. If the surgery is successful then I'll publish a paper and credit Gareth and West Manhattan Saints."

"How generous of you." Sam was very familiar with Janie and her family. Janie was one of his special patients and it broke his heart that she had a tumor that was ending her life. He didn't particularly like the fact that his mother was here and was planning on using poor Janie as a guinea pig to further her research.

"You're mad that I requested you," his mother said.

"I don't want anyone to know that you're my mother. You know that and you agreed to those conditions if you were to ever come here."

His mother snorted. "I really don't know why."

"I want to earn this fellowship on my own."

His mother snorted again and moved to sit behind her desk. "Really a waste."

"Pediatrics is a waste?"

"No."

"Then a waste of my talent?"

His mother shrugged. "I wouldn't know. I've never seen you operate, but given that you're my child I would assume that you have decent surgical abilities."

Sam rolled his eyes. "How generous of you to compliment me."

"You're being immature."

"Why did you request me?"

"To test your surgical abilities. Chief Langley speaks very highly of you and I want to see if you live up to his praise."

"I don't need to live up to anyone's expectations. I came here to learn under Dr. Chang."

His mother snorted. "You could be extraordinary. Brain surgery is cutting edge. If your abilities are as good as Gareth says they are then you're just wasting your talent in pediatrics. Do you want to settle for the ordinary?"

"Aye. I do."

His mother shook her head and then picked up a file, effectively dismissing him as she opened it up and began to read. "You're on my service. There's no point in arguing about it."

"I would rather not be."

"If you raise a stink don't you think people will question why you don't want to work with me?"

She had a point.

"Fine," he agreed grudgingly, but he was not happy. Not that she cared. His mother only cared about herself.

"Good. Well, if we're done talking I'd rather like to get to work."

"Of course, *Mother.*" Sam opened the door and barged out, slamming it behind him. As he turned around he crashed right into Mindy.

"Dr. Napier!" She gasped in surprise.

"I'm sorry, Dr. Walker. What're you doing here?"

"Bringing Dr. Hanley the information she requested on Baby C. Is she busy?"

"Yes, but I'm sure she'll want to see the file."

Mindy glanced up at him and frowned. "Are you okay, Sam?"

He frowned. "Perfectly."

He wanted to tell her he wasn't fine. That he was annoyed, but if he did then he would have to tell her that Dr. Hanley was his mother and then the whole story about his mother and Langley would come out.

The only people at West Manhattan Saints that knew about his situation were Langley and Dr. Chang. Sam knew that Dr. Chang wouldn't say anything and he thought Langley had enough couth not to say anything either.

After all, his mother had eventually made him a cuckold as well. Still, there was no reason to take it out on Mindy, but he really didn't want to get into it right now. He just had to go somewhere and calm down. Maybe do some charting in a broom closet.

"Are you sure you're okay?"

"I'm fine. Good day, Dr. Walker." He walked

away from her, brushing her off. It hurt him to do it, but it was for the best.

This kind of situation was why he didn't want to get involved with anyone he worked with. Messes like this. Rumors and secrets. He was here to practice medicine, not fall in love.

Who said anything about love?

Sam cursed under his breath.

He knew he had to get out of there and put some distance between him and his mother.

CHAPTER TEN

MINDY COULD FEEL all eyes on her as she carefully made an incision in her patient's uterus. Baby B's amniotic sac had broken and it was time to deliver the quintuplets. They had managed to last until thirty-two weeks.

Two weeks longer than when they'd had the meeting in the boardroom. Which was great, and the fluid around Baby C's brain remained stable, though he would still need a shunt. There were teams of neonatologists and pediatric doctors waiting to take the babies as she delivered them. She could see Sam standing there, waiting for Baby C. Once Baby C was delivered Sam was going to take him into the next OR where a shunt would be placed by Dr. Hanley.

Even though Dr. Hanley was a brilliant neurosurgeon, she was a bit of a narcissist.

Mindy took a deep calming breath as she continued to work. There were a lot of lives at stake and she didn't have time to worry about anyone else in this room.

"Delivering Baby A," she announced out loud, as she made the cut and gently removed Baby A from the uterus. She cut the cord and handed the baby to the waiting team. As Mindy focused on the next baby, she could hear the healthy scream of Baby A, who was being assessed under an islet table by Team A.

Mindy smiled, though no one could tell she was smiling under her surgical mask. She did love the sound of healthy lungs.

"Delivering Baby B."

The resident on Dr. Chang's team stepped forward with a blanket and Mindy cut the cord and placed the baby in team B's care. Then headed to her problem baby.

"Delivering Baby C."

Sam stepped forward, waiting to take his charge. He winked at her from behind the mask in an encouraging way as she quickly delivered Baby C.

Sam took the little guy and whisked him off to a warming table to check his vitals before they took him into surgery.

Mindy stopped for a moment. Just a moment, but didn't hear a cry from Baby C.

Come on, little guy. Come on.

Then there was a weak wail from across the OR.

"How is he, Dr. Napier?" Mindy called out, as she cauterized a bleeder quickly so she could move on to the other babies.

"Weak. His vitals aren't good and he has some apparent hydrocephalus. Taking Baby C to OR two."

Mindy glanced up briefly to see Baby C being hooked up to monitors and ventilators, prepping him for his immediate surgery. Such a hard start to life.

"Delivering Baby D," she called out, as she removed the tiny baby. Baby D had some breathing issues, but Mindy couldn't worry about that as she finished up and moved on to Baby E. The final baby.

As much as she was thinking about the babies and all those fragile little lives in different teams' hands, she couldn't think about them. She had to focus on the mom's health, so that she could recover and take care of all those babies.

She'd controlled the whole procedure as far as she could by setting the teams. As much as she wanted to hover over all those precious lives, she had to step back and let go. She had to let the teams she'd picked take over.

It was a perk of having her practice in a hospital setting that she knew the surgeons and could handpick them. When her practice was private and out of the office, she left that decision up to the neonatologist team, which stressed her out.

This way was better.

"Delivering Baby E." She handed the little girl to team E and now she had to make sure Mom was okay and stitched up. "Add Syntocinon to her IV."

"Yes, Dr. Walker." The anesthesiologist added the meds.

Mindy went to work on repairing bleeders and then finally was able to remove the placentas. Once they were gone she could work on closing up the uterus. "Good work, Dr. Walker."

Mindy glanced up to see Dr. Chang standing beside her.

"Is everything okay with your team?"

"Perfect. My team can handle Baby B. She's on her way to the NICU. I wanted to observe, if that's okay?"

"Of course."

Mindy worked diligently to check the uterus, to make sure nothing of the five separate placentas had been left behind. If anything remained it could pose a serious infection risk to the mother.

Once she'd checked and made sure everything was intact and healthy, she began to close up the uterus.

"Dr. Chang, they need you in OR two. It's Baby C."

Dr. Chang glanced back at the nurse who had come in. "Can't Dr. Hanley handle a shunt?"

"There are some more complications to Baby C and Dr. Hall is dealing with Baby E."

Mindy glanced up and Dr. Chang nodded to the nurse.

"I'll be there in a moment." Dr. Chang turned to Mindy. "Don't worry, we'll take care of him. Dr. Napier is in there."

"I know the baby is in good hands."

Dr. Chang nodded and left.

Focus.

Sam and Amelia were more than capable of helping Baby C. Both of them were brilliant surgeons. Baby C was in good hands.

Still, a sense of dread settled over her and she glanced at the mother, who was still under general anesthesia, and she felt a pang of heartache for her. When Mrs. Jameson woke up she wasn't going to be able to hold her babies and then she would have to tell her that one of those babies needed a bit more medical care.

It was the least favorite part of her job.

Mindy sighed and continued closing up Mrs. Jameson so they could get her into Recovery.

After her job was done she could check on the babies.

She could see a long night in her future but she didn't mind in the least.

Sam stood in the critical level of the NICU. Baby C, who had been named Michael, was critically ill.

The shunt placement had gone fine, but then he developed pulmonary hypertension and was currently on a ventilator, helping him to breathe.

Last night his bowel had perforated, which was common with premature babies.

Sam hadn't left Michael's side. He felt responsible for him. Sam was the resident on his case and Dr. Chang, Dr. Hall and his mother had many other patients they had to deal with so they couldn't hang about.

Really, he shouldn't be either, but he couldn't help himself. When it came to babies who were so ill… At least Maya hadn't been this ill when he'd dealt with her.

Michael, on the other hand…

Sam glanced furtively at the monitor, watching Michael's vitals, which told him that the poor little guy was struggling.

"Come on, buddy," he mumbled under his breath.

"Why are you still here?"

Sam spun around to see his mother enter Michael's private room. "I'm monitoring my patient."

"There are capable NICU nurses who can do that." His mother moved around to the incubator.

"I'm very well aware of that." Sam stepped back to allow his mother to open the incubator and examine the baby.

"Incisions look good."

"Aye," Sam remarked. "There's nothing wrong with the shunt placement."

His mother smiled. "Of course there isn't."

Sam rolled his eyes.

"You did good in my OR," his mother said. "I'd like you to aid in my surgery with Janie."

"Why?"

"I'm offering you a chance at something brilliant, rather than standing here staring at a monitor."

"I'm monitoring my patient," he said through gritted teeth.

His mother shook her head. "Call it what you will, but I don't think you'll be standing here much longer."

"What's that supposed to mean?"

"Samuel, I raised you better than that. Look at the vitals. Baby C won't make it through the night."

It was like a slap across the cheek.

"You're wasting your time in pediatrics. Switch to neurosurgery. I didn't pay for your education to waste it on children."

"You're not a pediatric surgeon," Sam snapped.

"See the facts, Sam."

"Michael, not Baby C, will do just fine."

His mother shook his head. "You're throwing away your talent, wasting your time here."

"Neurosurgery has a high mortality rate as well," Sam snapped.

"What does that have to do with anything?"

"You seem to be implying that I'm wasting my time with children who are just going to die anyway."

"That's not what I was implying. Honestly, Samuel, what I meant was what can you do to prevent his death by standing here, staring at a monitor? You should be working on your surgical skills. Not standing here."

"So you've mentioned."

"So?" his mother asked.

"What?"

"Are you going to continue to stand here?"

"Aye," Sam snapped.

His mother shook her head again and left the NICU room. Sam cursed under his breath. His mother was absolutely impossible. She wasn't much of an optimist, but when he stared at the monitors again he knew that his mother was probably right.

He clenched his fists and wanted to hit something, wanted to scream.

"Dr. Napier, what're you still doing here?" Dr. Chang asked as she walked into the room.

"I…I don't know." Sam ran his fingers through his hair. "What's his prognosis?"

Dr. Chang sighed. "It's not good. He's got a lot of cards stacked against him."

Sam stared down at the little baby, struggling to live. "He can turn a corner. I've seen worse."

"I know. He can, but…I don't think so," Dr. Chang sighed. "There's nothing more you can do here. The parents will be coming up soon. I'm going to talk about options."

"Can I stay?"

"No. Go home, Sam. You've done all you can do."

Sam nodded, even though he didn't want to leave. For some reason he felt responsible for this child. Like if he was more extraordinary he could've saved the child's life, but his mother had made it clear that he wasn't. He was only ordinary.

His mother had made that clear.

As he stood in the hall Michael's mother, Mrs. Jameson, was wheeled past him. She didn't notice him there, but the look on her face spoke volumes. Mrs. Jameson already knew what was going on. She knew why Dr. Chang was calling her into Michael's room.

Sam hovered, watching through the window as Dr. Chang knelt down, placing a hand on Mrs. Jameson's knee as she broke the news.

Mrs. Jameson hunched over, her face in her hands, her shoulders shaking. Sam's heart clenched and he could feel tears sting his own eyes. How did parents deal with it? It was something he had never understood, but he admired them for it.

Admired the hours spent by bedsides. The hope, then watching hope dashed and seeing sorrow replace it was too much for him. Especially today.

I want to save them all.

He'd been pushed to his breaking point and he began to question himself. Could he handle this?

He used to be able to handle this. So what had changed?

Mindy.

Before she'd come along he'd managed to keep his emotions in check. Nothing had fazed him. He hated to see children suffer and when they died it hurt him, but none had affected him like this one and it was all Mindy's fault.

Somehow, some way she'd got him to open up and he didn't like it one bit.

He had to get out of there.

Sam left West Manhattan Saints as fast as he could, but instead of taking the subway back to his flat in Brooklyn he walked toward her apartment.

The doorman wasn't on duty and he slipped in after holding the door open for an elderly man exiting.

Sam was on autopilot as he hit the button to the penthouse floor and in what seemed like a

New York minute he was standing in front of her door, knocking.

Mindy opened the door. "Sam? What're you doing here?"

"Don't speak."

"What—?" He cut her off by taking her in his arms and kissing her.

Mindy was shocked that Sam had shown up at her door. The last time she'd seen him had been in Michael's room in the NICU. He'd been staring down into the incubator, looking heartbroken.

She wanted to reach out to him, because it was obvious that he was hurting. Ever since the surgery three days ago he'd been different. Withdrawn, almost downtrodden, and she didn't know why.

So, instead of going to him, she'd walked away. Besides, it was better that way. He wouldn't have appreciated her consoling him at work and it wouldn't have been good for her either. She couldn't let him into her heart and if she'd gone to him in that NICU he would've broken down all the careful walls protecting her. So she had let him be.

Now she was wrapped up in his arms and he was kissing her. A kiss that made her knees knock together.

The kiss ended and she had to lean against his chest for a moment to get her bearings. Right now it felt like the world was spinning off kilter a bit.

"Can I come inside?"

Turn him away. Say no.

As she glanced up into those blue eyes, which were glazed over in lust, tenderness and pain, she found she couldn't resist him. She was so weak. And though her common sense told her not to, she wanted to trust him. She wanted him to fill that empty, raw spot in her heart. She wasn't sure she could, but she could have tonight.

And she wanted tonight.

So badly.

"Yes," she whispered.

He grinned, relieved. "Good."

Mindy tried to step to the side to let him in but instead he scooped her up in his arms and kicked her door shut with the heel of his shoe.

"Sam!" she gasped.

"I'm sorry. I can't help myself." He headed off in the direction of the bedroom.

"Sam," she whispered, as he nuzzled her neck.

"Do you want me to stop?"

"No."

"Good." He set her down on the bed, joining her. He leaned over her and a shiver of anticipation coursed through her.

This was wrong. So wrong.

And she didn't care one bit, because right here and now it was just the two of them. There was no one else. Here they were just Sam and Mindy.

He brushed his knuckles down the side of her face, his blue eyes twinkling in the dim light that filtered in through the crack in her drapes, just a bit of the city creeping in on them.

"You're so beautiful." Then he leaned down and pressed another kiss against her lips, light at first and then more urgent, as if he couldn't get enough of her. His body was pressed against hers and she was glad she wasn't wearing one of her skirts, so she could open her legs and let his weight settle between her thighs. Mindy arched her hips. She wanted him closer and she didn't want anything between them.

No clothes, no walls. Nothing. Just them.

Sam moaned. "Mindy, I want you."

"How much?"

Sam kissed her again, his tongue pushing past her lips, entwining with hers, making her blood sing with need.

"So much." He ran his hand over her body, but clothes were in the way. She wanted his hands on her bare flesh.

Mindy pushed him away.

"Have you changed your mind?" he asked.

"No." She sat up and took off her baggy T-shirt. "I want you naked." And she reached for the belt on his trousers, undoing it and slowly pulling it out of the belt loops. She then went for the button at the top of his pants. Sam moaned as her hand slipped underneath to touch him, just for a moment.

They made quick work of their clothes, until they were both naked. Nothing between them.

"I've tried so hard to resist you," Sam whispered against her neck. "But I can't. I need you again."

"I want you too, Sam."

She wanted him to erase her past. She wanted him to help her forget. When she was in his arms she wasn't that meek wallflower she had been in California and she wasn't a surgeon. She was just Mindy. Sexy, desirable Mindy, and she loved that he made her feel that way. No man had ever made her feel that way before.

"I want you so badly."

His lips captured hers in a kiss, silencing any more words between them. Mindy pulled him down. His body pressed against hers. It was just them, exposed and vulnerable to each other. His hands slipped down her sides, trailing over her flesh in little circles.

"So beautiful," he murmured.

It drove her wild and made her blood heat. His fingers found their way up to her breast, circling around her nipple, teasing. She sighed.

"So beautiful," he said again. "You drive me wild."

She ran her fingers through his hair as he began to kiss her again, but just light kisses starting at the lips and training lower, down over her neck. Lingering at her breasts, he used his tongue to tease her. She arched her back as pleasure shot through her again.

"I love it when you moan like that."

"Do you?" Mindy asked dreamily.

"Aye."

"Why?"

"Because when you moan like that I know you want me just as much as I want you." He took one nipple in his mouth and gently sucked for a moment. "Tell me how much you want me."

"So bad," she whispered.

His hand moved between her legs and he began to stroke her. Mindy cried out and then, when his hand was replaced by his mouth and tongue, it made her topple over the edge. She tried to stop herself from coming, but she couldn't. It was too much. It was a pleasure she'd never experienced before.

As she came down from her climax Sam moved away.

"Where are you going?" There was a definite shake to her voice.

"Hold on." He searched his trouser pocket and pulled a condom out. "I didn't think you wanted me to continue without this."

"Good call." Mindy sat up, even though her legs felt a bit boneless. She took the condom packet from his hand.

"What're you doing?" Sam asked.

She pushed him down and straddled his legs. "Let me help you."

"I don't think that's…" He trailed off as she opened the wrapper and rolled it down over his shaft. Sam uttered a few choice Gaelic words as she stroked him.

"I love having you under me," she teased him, leaning over him and nibbling on his ear lobe.

"I'd rather have you under me." And before she knew what was happening he'd flipped her and was pressing her back down against the mattress, covering her with his body, spreading her legs and thrusting into her.

Mindy bit her lip to stop from crying out. She dug her nails into his shoulder as Sam filled her completely.

"You feel so good," he moaned. "So good."

She moved her hips, encouraging him to move, but he just chuckled.

"Why are you teasing me?" she asked.

"I want you to beg." He began to nibble her neck. "Beg for it."

"Please."

"Please, what?"

"I want you, Sam. Please, make love to me."

He moaned. "As you wish."

Sam moved slowly at first, taking his time, but she wanted so much more of him she urged him to go faster until he lost control and was thrusting against her hard and fast. Soon another coil of heat unfurled deep within her, pleasure overtaking her as he brought her to another climax. Only this time they were joined as one. This time when she came it would be around him, it would be with him, and that's what she wanted most.

She wrapped her legs around him, holding him tight against her, urging him on. Sam cried out as he came and she held him until he collapsed against her. Mindy ran her hand down his neck, his pulse racing under her fingertips.

What have I done?

She knew and she didn't care. She wanted Sam. She wanted him to make her forget about the pain and humiliation she'd endured in California.

She wanted to feel again. Mindy had thought that their one-night stand would make her feel again and though it had been good, it hadn't changed her. Not the way tonight had. There had been more to tonight. A connection she couldn't quite explain, or perhaps she didn't want to explain because she wasn't ready to admit it to herself.

Either way, tonight when Sam had come to her, so vulnerable and full of emotion, she'd felt alive again. Like she wasn't just a spent force. She'd felt desirable. Sexy. Dean had never made her feel that way before he'd admitted to himself that he was gay.

In fact, no other man had made her feel like Sam did.

She wished they could stay like this forever, but they couldn't. Tears stung her eyes, but only for a moment, and she got them under control. Mindy wasn't ready for Sam to see her cry yet. She wasn't ready to show that weakness, that flaw in her.

Right now she just wanted to savor the moment of being with him. Their bodies pressed together, limbs entwined, hearts racing.

It felt so good, being with him. Too good almost and that was a dangerous thing. Sam was supposed to be off-limits and it was obvious that she couldn't resist him.

She'd tried and failed.

Sam kissed her gently on the lips, his fingers

stroking her face as she ran her hands down over his back. He rolled away from her and propped himself up on one elbow, those blue eyes twinkling with tenderness.

"Don't go yet."

A sly smile played on his lips. "What makes you think I was going somewhere?"

"The last time you moved away I fell asleep and when I woke up you were gone. I want you right here."

"The last time we were together it was a one-night stand between strangers." He leaned over and kissed her again. "You taste so good."

"Stay. Please."

"I'm not going anywhere yet."

She rolled over on her side and touched his face. She didn't want him to go. She didn't want this stolen moment to end. Not yet. She just wanted to remain here in this cocoon of happiness, where the outside world couldn't intrude. Where there were no nasty rumors, no sick people, no surgeries. Nothing. Just them. Just two people together.

"I want you again, Sam. I need you again."

He grinned lazily. "Let me catch my breath."

She cocked an eyebrow. "Oh, yes?"

"Yes, because I'm not done with you yet. Not by a long shot."

A zing coursed through her. *Oh, yes.* This was all so wrong, wanting him. So wrong that it felt so right.

CHAPTER ELEVEN

MINDY COULDN'T HELP but blush as Sam stroked her cheek. The last time they'd slept together she hadn't really known him so there had been no awkward moment afterwards. It had saved a bit of embarrassment, a bit of giggling, and then she did grin, because she was glad he was still here. She was glad it had happened.

This time it had been so much better because she liked Sam. She knew Sam. He was more than eye candy. More than just a one-night stand she'd picked up in a bar. She admired him. Respected him. He was her friend.

More than a friend.

She was falling for him. It thrilled and terrified her.

"You look quite pleased with yourself," Sam said.

"A bit." She tucked her arm under her pillow

and rolled onto her side. "So, what brought you to my door tonight?"

Sam grinned. "You need a justification?"

"I thought we were just going to be friends."

"I needed to see you. I just didn't know how much until you opened the door."

Mindy smiled. She knew he'd been stressed about Michael. For some reason Sam was taking Michael's medical condition very hard. Everyone had noticed by the way he'd hovered over the incubator for the first forty-eight hours of Michael's life. It was dedication, but Mindy had an inkling that it was something more.

"I'm glad you came to see me."

"Are you?"

"I am."

Sam rolled over and sat up, running his fingers through his hair. "This has been one heck of a week."

"What's going on? Something is bothering you and I think it's more than just an ill patient."

He sighed again. "It's hard for me to say. I don't tell many people."

He was hiding something from her and it made her nervous.

He's not Dean. Besides, she had her own secrets. "I get it."

He cocked an eyebrow. "You get what?"

"I get secrets and not wanting to share them."

"Do you?" he asked.

"Of course."

"You have secrets?"

Mindy shrugged. "There's not much to tell. I left California and an ex-husband behind."

"An ex-husband?" Sam asked.

"Yes." Her cheeks flushed with warmth and she couldn't believe she was actually telling Sam about Dean. "He cheated on me. I trusted him and he destroyed that trust." It was so hard to say the words. She didn't tell him that Dean had cheated on her with her best friend, but Sam was the first person in New York she'd told about Dean. She was trying so hard to hide that part of her life. It was so good to finally tell someone the hurt she'd buried for over a year.

Sam looked thoughtful and she worried it was too much information. That he'd leave or be embarrassed. Instead, he sighed wearily, "Dr. Hanley is my mother."

"Your mother?"

"Aye. She's my mother."

Now she was really shocked. Dr. Hanley was his mother? She didn't see a resemblance and she would've had no idea by the way they dealt with each other. She knew there was a vague disdain on Dr. Hanley's side, not unusual for a world-class surgeon who thought highly of herself, but a mother-son connection? That she would never have guessed. She'd known Sam's mother was a doctor, but Dr. Hanley? She hadn't pegged Dr. Hanley for the maternal type.

"You look like you've gone into shock."

"I guess I have a bit. Why were you keeping it a secret?" Mindy asked.

Sam sighed. "I'm not as extraordinary as her. Just ask her yourself."

"What?" Mindy asked confused. "Since when is she the expert on that?"

"I didn't want any favors in my career. I wanted to earn my place," Sam said. "I'm Dr. Napier. Not Dr. Hanley's son. Well, I am, but I'm not."

"You have something to prove. I get that. I respect it."

Sam smiled. "Aye, but do you really get it? You're a top-notch surgeon too."

"I do get it. It's why I left California."

"Because you got divorced?"

"Yes," Mindy said. "He was my partner in my practice. I trusted him, but after his betrayal came out I couldn't trust him. Not his opinions on patients, not in the OR. It would've been detrimental to my patients to continue on in that environment. It would've been detrimental to me to continue second-guessing myself."

"Your career means a lot to you."

Mindy nodded. "It does. Though I'm hardly a tough surgeon like your mom. I tend to wear my heart on my sleeve."

"That's not necessarily a bad quality. And

you are tough. You demand excellence and perfection."

"I do. I came here to do serious work."

"Are you implying I'm not serious work?"

Mindy laughed. "No."

"Am I a mistake?" he asked, running his hand over her cheek.

"I haven't figured that out yet."

Sam chuckled and then sobered up. "I promise you I'm not trying to sleep my way to the top."

Mindy's spine stiffened. "What're you talking about?"

"My mother. She slept her way to the top, breaking my father's heart. See, surgery and her career were more important than her marriage and me."

"I know you're not sleeping your way to the top, but what are we doing?"

Sam sighed. "I don't know."

"I don't think a relationship is on the cards."

Because she couldn't let it be. No matter how much she wanted it.

"I can't promise you anything."

It stung, but she'd known that all along. She knew that he couldn't offer her anything and she really couldn't offer him anything either. She was still finding herself, still rebuilding her life after what had happened with Dean.

This time was for her.

"I don't expect anything." She leaned over and kissed him on the lips. "I'm glad you came over tonight, though."

"Me too. Though I wish…"

"What?"

"Maybe my mother is right. Maybe if I was more extraordinary like her I could do more for Michael. His siblings are thriving; it makes no sense that he's not."

"You care for your patients. That's an extraordinary quality."

"Caring is not good enough." He rolled out of bed and started pulling on his clothes.

"Where are you going?" she asked.

"Back to the hospital."

"Sam, there's nothing more you can do. Standing over Michael's incubator won't do anything to help him. Stay here. Rest."

He smiled at her. "It's best I leave. Besides, if I get back into that bed I'm not going to rest."

A zing shot through her body and she blushed again at his suggestion. He was right. He couldn't spend the night here. What had happened here between them tonight was a secret. No one else could know because it could ruin both of their reputations.

"You'd better go, but promise me you won't go back to the hospital." She knew it was futile. She knew he was going back to the hospital. He was dedicated. It was another thing she loved about him.

Loved?

No, that couldn't be. She wasn't ready and he was off limits, but Sam was so easy to be with and it scared her to death.

What am I doing? She didn't know.

"What's wrong?" Sam asked, as he finished buttoning his shirt.

"What do you mean?" Mindy asked.

"Something changed. Your demeanor."

"Nothing," she said.

"No, it's something."

"It's nothing." Who was she kidding? It was. It was turning into something fast and she was scared.

Sam knew it was something, even though she was denying it. Something had changed. They'd been having an easy conversation and then her walls had gone up again. Maybe it was something he'd done, but then when he'd told her he couldn't promise her any more than what had happened between them she had still been amiable.

"Well, I think I'll head out."

Mindy nodded, but would barely look at him. "I'll see you in the morning. You're on my service again."

"Unless I'm forced to work on my mother's."

Mindy's head snapped up. "What?"

Sam sighed and sat down on the edge of the bed. "She's demanding that I join her in the

OR for her experimental surgery on one of Dr. Chang's patients."

"The brain surgery."

"Yes."

"Well, are you familiar with the patient?" Mindy asked.

"Yes. Very."

"Then it makes sense."

He frowned. "You're taking her side?"

"No, but I do see why she would want you on the case if you're familiar with the patient and she's not."

Sam snorted. "That's never stopped her before and, besides, I won't do much in her OR. She never allows her residents to get their hands dirty."

"Are you trying to tell me to keep you busy so you don't end up in her OR?"

Sam snorted again. "I doubt you can stop her."

"Why? I'm an attending as well."

"Because she'll go to Langley." And he would grant his mother her wish because he was wrapped around his mother's little finger. *Don't think about it.*

"Ah," Mindy said, nodding. "Yes, he'll likely cave to a well-known surgeon over me."

Or cave to a woman he slept with.

Only he didn't say that thought out loud. Mindy didn't need to know that. It was embarrassing. Shameful. And he was doing the same here with Mindy. Though he tried to tell himself otherwise. He cared for Mindy and his mother didn't seem to care about anyone but herself.

They were different.

Were they?

That thought made his stomach twist.

"Well, I'd better go."

Mindy nodded. "Okay. I'll see you tomorrow."

"Right." Sam lingered, wondering if she'd lean over and kiss him, but she didn't and maybe that was for the best. He saw himself out of her penthouse and headed out onto the street. He had every good intention of heading back to Brooklyn, just like when he'd originally left the hospital and instead had ended up at Mindy's place and in her arms.

Her warm, soft arms.

He fought the urge to turn back. He couldn't go back, because he didn't want to hurt her, because he didn't want to promise her something that he couldn't give her.

He never wanted to hurt her. He didn't want to be like his mother.

Instead, he headed back to the hospital to torture himself further. He wanted to be there by Michael's bedside if he passed on. Sam felt it was his duty to be by his patient's side. Although it pained him to watch a child lose the battle for life, he wanted to be there. To say goodbye.

When he walked into the residents' locker room his phone rang. It was Kimberlyn.

"You know what time it is?" Sam teased, as he answered the call from his former roommate.

"Why are you answering, then?" she teased.

"Why not?"

"Where are you?" she asked.

"I went back home to sleep and now I'm back at the hospital."

Kimberlyn snorted. "I don't believe that for a second."

"Why? You're how many miles away? You don't know what I'm doing."

"There's no way you could've caught a subway, slept and come back in the amount of time you were gone."

"Fine. I didn't go home." Sam put his phone on hands-free and pulled off his shirt, then pulled on his scrubs.

"Where are you? You're all echoey."

"That's none of your business, Mother."

Kimberlyn snorted. "Great. You're in the locker room and probably getting naked. Nasty. I thought you were off? You should go home and sleep."

"I've been busy. So you've called to nag me. I have to say I've missed it."

Kimberlyn chuckled. "Me too. I called because I felt like I should and I'll be up your way in a few days. We're visiting Enzo's parents."

"Good." Sam was pleased. "I have to go."

"So do I. I'm headed home, though not to get hot and heavy with Enzo, who is on duty tonight. Where are you headed?"

"Back up to the NICU."

"I miss nagging you," she sighed. "I'll talk to you later."

"Yes." They said a few more words and he hung up. He pulled on his lab coat, shut his locker and then made his way to the NICU. The NICU was still dark, just a few nurses and a neonatologist fellow going from room to room, but it was quiet.

He liked the NICU. He liked the quiet, except for tonight. It was too quiet. He headed into Michael's room and over to the incubator, peering down at the little guy struggling to live.

Live.

Sam sighed and pulled up a chair, grabbing Michael's chart. "Well, I hope you don't mind the company tonight, buddy."

He flipped open the chart, read the last stats

and smiled. They'd improved. Michael's stats had actually improved.

"You're back?"

Sam looked up and saw Dr. Chang. "You're still here?"

"It's my night to do a twenty-four-hour shift. You haven't answered why you've come back. I thought you left?"

"I did for a bit. Just walked around. His stats are better."

Dr. Chang smiled. "They are. He's still in danger but he's turned a bit of a corner."

"What did you tell the parents?"

"I gave them options, they're still thinking about them. Of course, if Michael is getting stronger they probably won't have to worry about them." Dr. Chang stood on the other side of the incubator and smiled down at the little baby. "Dr. Walker is an excellent surgeon."

Sam's stomach flipped over. Did she know? "Yes, she is. I've learned a lot from her."

Dr. Chang glanced up at him. "I'm sure you have."

"What's that supposed to mean?"

Dr. Chang cocked an eyebrow. "What are you implying? I mean you must've learned a lot from such a skilled surgeon. Nothing more. Should I be concerned?"

"No. I just...with my mother being here..."

Dr. Chang snorted. "Enough said."

"How do you feel about her working on Janie?"

He could tell by Dr. Chang's expression, her furrowed brow and the tense way she stood that she wasn't too keen on it. "Janie's parents approved of the surgery. They weren't coerced. Janie is terminal. If the procedure works then Janie may get more time."

Sam nodded. He'd expected that answer from Dr. Chang. She was quite diplomatic. He admired that about her.

"Are you going to stay here?" Dr. Chang asked.

"I think so."

"Catch up on your filing, then. I'll send an intern in with your charts. Print neatly, your writing is atrocious." She winked and then left the NICU.

Sam laughed and set Michael's file back, before leaning back in the rocking chair. He hoped that his mother didn't force him to work on her surgery. He hoped she picked another resident so rumors wouldn't begin to fly.

He'd rather work with Mindy on her service. His blood heated as he thought of Mindy and the fact he'd left her again, naked in bed. At least this time he hadn't had to sneak off. They had talked, laughed, until she'd closed herself off again. Of course, he'd thrown up his own walls too.

It was for the best.

CHAPTER TWELVE

MINDY FINISHED ROUNDING on her patients in the maternity ward and sent off the two interns she'd been assigned to do various labs and tests. She was surprised that Sam hadn't shown up for his rounding. It wasn't like him.

Maybe he's avoiding me.

And she hated thinking that. Sam wasn't Dean.

Perhaps his mother got hold of him?

It was clear from their conversation that Sam and his mother didn't have the best relationship, but there was more to it than that. Then again, she hadn't told him everything. She'd just glossed over why she didn't want a relationship.

It was a pathetic excuse now that she thought about it.

Still, it was for the best. She knew the other attendings were all going to vote that Sam get one of the pediatric fellowships. He'd proved his worth to them long before she'd shown up, but she didn't feel like she could cast a vote.

Not after last night.

Mindy bit her lip, nervous about how to approach it because she didn't want rumors to start flying around about her and Sam.

That would ruin her reputation here and could really mess up Sam's career.

I don't want to leave and find a new place.

Dean had called her a coward the day before she'd left for New York because she'd felt too embarrassed to face her problems, and maybe he was right.

Being bullied as a young girl and pushed around on her residency, well, she didn't really have a thick skin. Or not as thick as some others did.

She couldn't have a vote on the fellowship. It wouldn't be right.

Mindy put the chart of her last patient away behind the nursing station on the OB/GYN floor and headed over to Pediatrics. She had to speak to Dr. Chang and then Professor Langley. She wouldn't tell them why she was withdrawing her vote, only that she couldn't make a proper decision because she hadn't been here long enough.

Hopefully they would understand, without asking her to explain too much.

She was glad about what had happened between her and Sam; she cared about him a great deal and she didn't want to ruin his career. He was going to make a fine pediatric surgeon.

As she crossed through the NICU she paused to check on the progress of the quints, speaking briefly with the neonatologist nurses before heading to the level three NICU, where Michael was being cared for.

She swiped her identification card and entered the critical care NICU. Michael's room was the first room in that area of the NICU. She peered through the glass and saw Sam fast asleep in the rocking chair next to the incubator.

So that's why he hadn't answered his page or made rounds.

Mindy smiled as she watched him, her heart

melting a bit to see his dedication to children, to his patient. Why couldn't they have met at a different time? Why couldn't she have met him first instead of Dean? Why did she have to be his boss?

Life wasn't fair.

Look at poor Michael struggling to live while his four other siblings did well. That wasn't fair. She turned to leave but then went into the room to wake Sam. They may not ever have a relationship but she couldn't let him sleep the day away. He was late for rounds.

"Rise and shine," she called out, as she shut the door behind her.

Sam jumped up. "What time is it?"

"Nine o'clock in the morning."

Sam cursed under his breath. "I'm sorry. I can't believe I completely missed rounds like that."

"Your interns were wondering what happened when they showed up and you didn't."

"Great, they're going to think I'm a slacker."

Sam stood and stretched. "I'm sorry for missing rounds, Dr. Walker."

"It's fine, Sam."

"No, it's not fine. The decision is coming soon about the fellowship. I can't be slacking off now."

"It's not like you were in an on-call room or at your apartment. You were with a patient," Mindy offered.

"You're being too easy on me, Dr. Walker." Sam sighed. "I don't want you to be easy on me just because…"

"Don't finish that sentence," Mindy said. "I'm not being easy on you just because of what happened last night. Last night was a mistake."

Sam frowned. "Right. Well, I'm sorry nonetheless."

Mindy nodded. "Besides, I'm withdrawing my vote."

He cocked an eyebrow. "Why would you be doing that, then?"

"I don't think it's really fair of me to give an opinion now. If someone found out then it would have bad repercussions. Surgery is a very competitive career."

"Aye, I know. Why don't you vote for someone else, then?"

"Besides all that we've been through, you're the best and you deserve it."

Sam's cheeks tinged red. "Thank you, but there are two positions."

"I can't vote for someone I don't have confidence in. I can make one vote for the other spot, but I can't for the spot that's rightfully yours. So I won't vote for either."

"How are you going to get out of that?" He asked.

"I have my ways."

Sam nodded. "I appreciate it."

Mindy smiled. "I don't regret what happened between us, but I don't want it to ruin our careers. I really don't want to leave another practice."

"I don't know why you ran from California. You weren't in the wrong. Your ex is the one who wronged you."

"It was just easier," Mindy said quickly, because she didn't want to talk about it. Yeah, maybe she had been a bit of a coward for running away. She was the surgeon who'd made the most money in the practice, she was the one who'd brought in the most clients, but she'd been unable to stay in California. She couldn't be around Dean and Owen. Most of all, she didn't like that people saw her differently. New York was a clean slate and that's the way it was going to stay.

"Straighten yourself out and report to the OB/GYN floor. Your interns are currently running amok down there."

Sam nodded. "I will and thank you, Mindy."

She smiled and left the NICU.

Mindy eventually found Dr. Chang in her office. She gently rapped on the door.

"Can I speak to you for a moment?" she asked.

Dr. Chang looked up. "Of course, Dr. Walker. Come in."

Mindy shut the door and sat down in a chair. "I want to talk to you about my vote."

"Ah, yes, I was hoping you would come by and let me know. I'm hoping to announce my decision next week to the board of directors."

"I want to withdraw."

Dr. Chang looked confused. "Withdraw?"

Mindy nodded. "I haven't worked here long enough to determine who would be most deserving of the fellowship spots. I know that Dr. Powers made her recommendations before she left, but I don't think I can really give one."

Dr. Chang tented her fingers and leaned back in her chair. "I understand that. Thank you for coming to me with your concerns. Most surgeons wouldn't; they would be arrogant enough to think they can vote."

"I'm not that arrogant, I'm afraid," Mindy said.

"I know." Dr. Chang smiled. "It's one of the reasons I like you. My dealings with most OB/GYNs who specialize in the field of maternal-fetal medicine think they are God's gift to surgeons."

Mindy chuckled. "That sounds about right."

"Don't get me wrong. They have every right

to. I do know it's a fairly new field of medicine and each advancement saves lives. By all rights, you have the right to swagger a bit."

"Perhaps, but that's not my style. I keep a fairly low profile and do my duty to my patients."

Dr. Chang smiled. "As do I. Which is why I like you."

"Thank you. The feeling is mutual."

"So. How long have you and Sam been involved?"

The question caught Mindy completely off guard. She was going to deny it, but what was the point? "How did you know?"

"I read people. I can tell when people lie to me, but I also know when people are sneaking about."

"I can tell you we're not involved."

Dr. Chang nodded. "But…?"

"Before I started work here I went to a bar. Picked up a man and had a one-night stand. I had no idea it was Sam and he had no idea who I was."

"Ah, that makes sense."

"There's nothing more to tell. Nothing further will happen. I don't want to risk his career, he's a brilliant surgeon."

"He is." Dr. Chang smiled. "Thank you for being so honest. It won't leave these walls. I like Sam and I want him to work with me. He has so much potential."

"In spite of what his mother thinks?"

Dr. Chang chuckled. "Agreed. So he told you. Well, that's good. Honestly, I don't know how much longer he'll be able to keep that secret from the rest of the hospital. That woman may be a brilliant neurosurgeon but she has no couth when it comes to name-dropping."

"I noticed. I take it you don't like *that* woman much either."

Dr. Chang grinned. "Ah, yes. Well, we were residents together. I found her quite annoying and what she did to her husband and Sam… There's no excuse for that. No excuse for cheating and breaking apart your family in such a callous way, but you didn't hear that from me."

"I won't say a word."

"He doesn't like it brought up. I admire him for not seeking favors or using his mother's name to gain footing. He may be a bit of a lone wolf here but everything he gets, every advance, every surgery he earns on his own merit."

"He told me as much," Mindy said.

Only Mindy wasn't sure that Sam quite believed that. His mother's shadow loomed over him. Even if people didn't know that Sam and Dr. Hanley were related, there was something holding him back, even if he didn't want to admit it.

Of course, there were things she didn't want to admit either. There were things she wanted to remain locked away. Everyone had their secrets, but relationships didn't work when there were secrets.

Mindy stood up. "Thank you for understanding, Dr. Chang, and I appreciate your discretion."

"Thank you for your honesty, Dr. Walker. You know the hospital doesn't frown on relationships between attendings?"

"I'm afraid I do, and it's for personal reasons."

Dr. Chang nodded. "I respect that." She reached across the desk and Mindy shook her hand. She left Dr. Chang's office but didn't feel any better. She was glad that she didn't have to have a say in the fellowship this time around and she was glad to get the truth out in the open with a colleague she admired. One who respected Sam as well, one who wouldn't do any damage to his career. It felt like a huge weight had been lifted off her shoulders and even though the stress of being discovered was gone, something still didn't feel quite right because even though she wouldn't date Sam, even though nothing could go any further, she wanted it to.

Try as she may, Mindy had fallen in love with Sam and it made her sad that nothing could happen between them.

Sam gritted his teeth as he made his way to the OR floor. He was on the pediatric floor when he saw that they were prepping Janie for surgery and then he got the page to head down to

OR three. He'd managed to avoid his mother for two days, but now, with them prepping Janie, he knew she'd be paging him.

When he got down there he was going to pass on the surgery. Even though it was Janie and he liked the family, he wasn't going to work with his mother. He just didn't have the patience to be in her presence today.

When he got down to the surgical floor, his mother was already in the OR.

Of course. Now I have to scrub in.

It was one of her little tricks. She was avoiding him, ignoring his texts about wanting to talk about the upcoming surgery because she knew he was going to turn her down. It was a game his mother liked to play. It was immature and Sam hated it, but he was used to it.

He entered the scrub room and glanced through the window into the OR to see his mother speaking to a few reporters, who were garbed and waiting anxiously for the surgery to start. At least poor Janie wasn't lying there while all this nonsense was going on. It just seemed to be the surgical team prepping for surgery, while his mother and Langley spoke to the press.

Great. Just what I need.

Both the people responsible for breaking his father's heart in the same OR and they wanted him to assist? Well, he would assist. He would just stand by and maybe suction the odd bleeder.

He finished scrubbing and headed into the OR, staying back near the doors waiting until his mother saw that he was there, but instead of her coming over Langley headed over to him.

"Why aren't you gowned, Dr. Napier?"

"I'm not planning on staying."

"Dr. Hanley requested your assistance."

"I'm well aware of that," Sam snapped.

"I would watch your tone with me. Now, go get gowned properly. The patient will be coming down soon."

He hated it when the man ordered him about like he was a child.

Don't let him get to you. That's what he kept telling himself, but he was losing the battle fast.

"I'm on Dr. Walker's rotation and I would prefer to stay there."

"I'm sure Dr. Walker won't mind you attending this surgery."

"I'm sure she wouldn't, but I would prefer to sit out all the same." Sam turned to leave, but Langley stepped in front of him.

"You're staying here."

White-hot rage bubbled up in Sam. He didn't like the tone Langley was taking with him, as if he was a child. As if he was his father. Sam lost all rational thought at that moment and the dam burst.

"You're not my father! You may have slept with my mother when I was a child, but you don't have any right to order me about and I won't stand for hours in an OR with my mother." Then he realized what he'd said out loud to Langley. He was the chief of surgery. The room had gone quiet and then he saw the gallery was full. It was full of his fellow residents, who had heard him shouting.

Kimberlyn, who had come up to visit Enzo's

family, was in the gallery, in shock, and Holly's mouth was hanging open pretty wide, and standing in the back row was Mindy. She looked heartbroken for him, she was pitying him. He didn't want her pity. It tore out his heart.

"I'm sorry. I don't know—"

"What do you think you're doing?" his mother shrieked. Professor Langley stepped back, still in shock himself at what had happened.

"I don't…" Sam didn't know what to say, because right now, at this instant, his reputation was ruined. It was absolutely shattered.

"You're an ungrateful son. How dare you humiliate and attack the chief of surgery in my OR? How dare you turn down this opportunity from me? Do you know how many strings I had to pull to get you into this surgical program and to get you into the pediatric program with Dr. Chang? In case you weren't aware, you're not *that* extraordinary."

"No. I guess I'm not," Sam shouted. "I never asked you to assist me. I didn't want your help.

I didn't want to earn my accolades the way you did. Sleeping your way to the top."

"Get out of my OR," she shouted.

"With pleasure."

Sam marched through the scrub room, ripping off his surgical mask and scrubbing out quickly. Langley followed him out into the hallway.

"Dr. Napier, wait!" It was Langley who had followed him out. He didn't know why and he wasn't too impressed that he had.

Sam stopped and turned. "You'll have to scrub in again."

"I am aware of that."

"What do you want?" Sam demanded.

"What was that about?" Langley asked.

"I think it's obvious."

"Why did you apply for the surgical program here?" he asked. "You clearly loathe me."

"Because of Dr. Chang. I knew she was the best in pediatrics. If it wasn't for her, I wouldn't have touched West Manhattan Saints with a ten-foot pole."

Langley crossed his arms. "Because of me?"

"Yes. You ruined my parents' marriage."

The older man shook his head. "Your parents' marriage was ruined long before I hit the scene."

"Why did you sleep with her?" Sam asked.

"Should you really be prying into your mother's private life like that? Isn't that inappropriate?"

"Tell me. Why did you sleep with her? Why did you break up a marriage? You could've had anyone, but you decided to pursue a married woman."

"I loved her." There was sadness on Gareth Langley's face. It was apparent that his mother had hurt more than his father, but at this moment Sam didn't have any sympathy for Langley. He could've walked away.

Mother could've walked away too.

"So did my father," Sam snapped. "So did a lot of men."

Langley winced at that statement, because he knew it to be true. "Yes, and I do regret what happened."

"That's not good enough."

"She broke my heart too," Langley said.

"I don't care. And in case it's not clear for you, I'm tendering my resignation from the surgical program and West Manhattan Saints." He turned around and didn't wait for the professor to say anything further.

The word was out that Dr. Hanley was his mother, that she'd pulled strings to get him into the program. He hadn't got where he was on his own merit. It had all been his mother, begging people to take him.

Well, he could take a hint.

He didn't know exactly where he'd go. Perhaps back home to Scotland. He didn't know, he just knew that his time at West Manhattan Saints was at an end.

"Sam!"

He whipped around and saw Mindy chasing after him. He didn't want to see her, he didn't want her to see him like this, and he didn't need her pity. So he turned back around and kept on, but she caught up with him and grabbed his arm, stopping him.

"Sam, didn't you hear me?"

"Aye," he said tersely, not looking her in the eye. "What do you want? Are you coming to shatter the rest of my tattered reputation by calling me by my first name in the halls?"

Mindy let go of his arm. "Why are you angry with me?"

"I don't have time for this."

"You stood up to your mother. That's a good thing."

Sam snorted. "Is it really?"

"It is. Don't listen to her. You're an extraordinary surgeon in your own right. You deserve to be here."

"No. I don't. I got here on her ticket. That much was made clear."

"You're a fool to believe that!"

"A fool?" He shook his head. "I'm done with this conversation. I have my locker to clean out."

Mindy blocked his escape route and stood in front of him. "What?"

"I resigned."

"You did what?" she asked, shocked.

"I quit."

Her brow furrowed. "That's a foolish thing to do."

He snorted. "Look who's talking."

Mindy's eyes narrowed. "What is that supposed to mean?"

"You know what I mean."

"No, but I do know that running away from this is a coward's way out. So everyone knows now that Dr. Hanley is your mother and slept with the chief. Who cares? It's their problem. You're a fine surgeon. You shouldn't quit."

"Why not? You ran away from California when your husband cheated on you. I'm doing the same. I'm running away."

"I—I didn't run."

He'd hurt her. It killed him, but it was for the best. Love was too hard and uncertain and he wanted nothing to do with it, even though he did. It was just that he had nothing to give her.

Nothing, so it was best to cut the strings. Let her go.

Besides, she'd made it clear she couldn't give

him anything and he didn't want to end up with someone who would hurt him like his mother had hurt his father, or do the same to her.

"You did. So I am. I don't need any favors or forgiveness," Sam snapped.

"Well, you won't be getting any forgiveness, if that's what you want." Mindy turned on her heel and marched in the other direction.

Sam's heart twisted and he hated himself for doing that, because he loved her even though he didn't really know what love was himself. He just knew he'd fallen in love with Mindy, but there was no way he'd win her back now.

It was for the best this way.

Go after her.

Only he didn't chase after her, because he didn't deserve her.

He didn't deserve any of this.

CHAPTER THIRTEEN

Three days later

"GO AWAY! I don't want to talk." Sam was tired of the incessant knocking. Every one of his roommates had come by his door in the last three days to try and talk him into coming back because the cat was out of the bag. Even Kimberlyn and Enzo had dropped by to talk some sense into him.

Everyone was interested in the fact that Dr. Hanley was his mother and that his mother and Langley had once been an item.

All he wanted was to be left in peace to pack. He was going to head back home to Scotland, set up a family practice. He was licensed for that at least.

That's not what you wanted to do.

No, it wasn't the dream when he'd been becoming a doctor. He'd wanted to be a pediatric surgeon. He loved working with kids, saving their lives. That was his joy, but that was never going to happen.

At least he would be an ocean apart from his mother and Mindy.

His heart ached as he thought of Mindy again.

Well, at least with him gone she could practice her medicine in a relatively peaceful environment.

The knocking continued and Sam cursed under his breath. He set down the stack of books he was going through and crossed his small apartment, flinging open the door. He was expecting it to be Kimberlyn or Holly, since they were the most insistent door-knockers.

"What do you want?" He was stunned to see Dr. Chang standing in the hallway, in street clothes. "Dr. Chang?"

"I'm aware that you're busy, Dr. Napier, but can I come in?"

"Sure." Sam stepped to the side and Dr. Chang walked into his apartment.

"Nice place."

"Thanks." Sam was still stunned. "Why are you here, Dr. Chang?"

Dr. Chang set her purse down on his bed and then took a seat in one of the battered old leather wing chairs he had in his small makeshift sitting room.

"This is a comfortable chair." Then she crossed her arms and leaned back. "You're heading back to Scotland, I hear?"

"How did you hear that?"

"Your father called me."

Now it was Sam's turn to be stunned. "My dad called you?"

"Yes, he and my husband were friends when he was married to your mother back in the mists of time."

Sam perched on the edge of the other wing chair. "I didn't know that."

Dr. Chang shrugged. "Well, you do know that

your mother and I were in the same resident program. Along with Chief Langley."

Sam grumbled under his breath. "I'd rather you not bring up his name."

"I know he did something horrible. He pursued a married woman and broke up a family, but he did love her and he thought she loved him too."

Sam snorted. "My mother doesn't love anyone."

Dr. Chang smiled. "No, and Chief Langley found that out soon enough."

"I know my mother cheated on Langley, but I don't have much sympathy for him. After all, he was just doing a favor for my mother by accepting me into the program. I don't need his pity or her favors."

"You're stubborn, like her."

"I'm nothing like her," Sam snapped.

"You are, in some ways. Look, your mother in her eccentric, egotistical way may *think* that she pulled strings to get you into this program, but it wasn't Chief Langley who helped pick the interns for the program the year you entered. It was me."

"You?"

Dr. Chang nodded. "Me. The board trusts me more than Langley when it comes to West Manhattan Saints' surgical program. I'm the one who had the final say and what I saw in your application was high grades and glowing reference letters. There was no hesitation on my part to accept you into the surgical program. Despite what your mother says, you're far from ordinary. She's just too stubborn to see what a brilliant surgeon you are."

Sam didn't know what to say. He was stunned. From the moment he'd decided to pursue a career in medicine he'd thrown his whole self into practicing medicine, while his mother had watched from afar and nitpicked over his skills.

Perhaps she'd been worried that if Sam didn't make it, it would somehow look bad on her, and by controlling his specialty she would be able to keep him under her thumb. Only he hadn't chosen her specialty. So she'd gone about knocking his confidence, so that he would turn to neurosurgery and she would dazzle him with her surgical prowess.

"I've made a right mess of things."

"In your words, aye, you have."

"I don't think I can go back."

Dr. Chang's eyes narrowed as she frowned. "You really have no choice. I don't accept your resignation."

"You really don't have a choice. The chief of surgery… Langley makes that call."

"No, *you* don't have a choice." Dr. Chang stood and stared him down, though she was much shorter than him. "*I* chose you when you were an intern, Sam. I've been grooming you."

Sam was stunned. "Pardon?"

"I think you heard me. You have earned one of the fellowship spots. It was a no-brainer and since I really don't want to go back to the drawing board you really have no choice."

"Did Mindy vote for me?"

"No. She withdrew her consideration after she

told me what had transpired between the two of you."

Sam was shocked. "She told you?"

"She did and told me that what happened was unintentional. So even though she felt you were an extraordinary surgeon, she couldn't rightfully vote for anyone. Maternal-Fetal Medicine's vote for fellowship was based on Dr. Powers's notes before she retired."

Sam was still stunned. Mindy knew that he didn't like favors and she'd done the best thing she could for him and told her colleague that she'd slept with a resident. She'd put her own career and reputation in jeopardy, by telling Dr. Chang that their one-night stand had been just a coincidence.

You're an idiot.

Sam sank back down in his wing chair and scrubbed a hand over his face. "I've made a right *bourach* of this whole thing."

"I agree."

Sam glanced up at Dr. Chang. "I have to talk to Langley and my mother."

Dr. Chang nodded. "I would also talk to Dr. Walker, but I don't think I have to tell you that."

"No, you don't."

"So you'll be coming back to West Manhattan Saints?"

Sam grinned. "Aye."

"Good." She picked up her purse and went to leave, but turned. "Look, your mother does care for you in her own way. She never wanted to be a mother, but your father wanted you and kind of pressed his case. I'm sorry that your father was hurt and that you think that maybe a family doesn't work if you're a surgeon, but it can. As long as both parties are willing."

"So you think maybe if my father hadn't made my mother have me, their marriage might've worked?"

"No, they were two different people. What I was saying wasn't implying that you should blame yourself for their break-up. I think they would've eventually gone their separate ways anyway. What I was trying to say was that your mother cares in her own way. She just doesn't know how to apologize. She doesn't know how to love."

Sam nodded. "I get it."

"I'm glad you do." Dr. Chang left his apartment, closing the door behind her.

Sam got up and stared out the window, watching Dr. Chang as she left the brownstone and headed to her car parked on the street.

He'd been so influenced by his parents' failed marriage, only seeing the one side because he had been there the day his father's heart had been crushed. All he'd seen had been the evil man who had stolen his mother away.

Sam had never once thought that his mother had been at fault for it all or that his dad had caused undue strain and hurt his mother as well by trying to make her something she wasn't.

He'd never wanted to hurt Mindy, but he had by implying that she was a coward for running away, and yet he'd planned to do the same thing.

He was the coward.

Mindy had risked her reputation to make sure

that he got what he deserved, and he'd thrown it all away.

Dr. Chang had a successful marriage and children. One day he could as well. He didn't have to be alone to be successful. For his mother, yes, but him? No, he didn't need to sentence himself to that lifestyle.

He'd make it right with Mindy and if she didn't want his heart then he deserved it, but he was going to make sure that she knew he was staying at West Manhattan Saints and she was going to stay as well. He wasn't going to let her run because he would make sure everyone knew that what had happened had been his fault.

There was a knock at the door and Kimberlyn poked her head in and Enzo was loitering in the hall. "Hey, I take it you're staying?"

Sam glanced over his shoulder. "Aye."

"Good." She smiled. "Because if you hadn't listened to Dr. Chang and changed your mind we were going to hog-tie you to make you stay."

Sam chuckled. "No need for hog-tying. I'm

staying and I think I'll head over to the hospital now and rectify that."

Rectify it all.

It took Sam over an hour to get to the hospital. He wasn't even sure if Mindy was on duty, but right now he was going to confront his mother and he owed the professor an apology. He headed up to the floor where his mother's office was.

He could see her shadow through the blinds.

Sam took a deep calming breath and knocked.

"Come."

He opened the door and shut it behind him.

"Well, I didn't expect to see you again, to be honest," his mother said casually.

"I know."

"I thought you were going to Scotland?"

"I changed my mind. How did you know about Scotland?"

"Your father."

Sam cocked an eyebrow. "You talked to Dad?"

"Yes." She tented her fingers and leaned back

in her chair. "Is there something you want to say to me?"

"I'm sorry that you felt the need to pull strings for me, to watch out for me, but really I'm not a failure. I won't bring shame to you."

His mother was visibly stunned. "Oh."

"I *am* an extraordinary surgeon. Professor Langley didn't pick me for this program. Dr. Chang did, and it was based on my own merits. I will make a fine pediatric surgeon."

"Are you looking for me to apologize?"

Sam shook his head. "No. I'm not. I don't need your validation and you don't need to apologize for my life. I may have been angry with you for a long time about Dad, but I can tell it was for the best. For all parties."

"Are you looking for my approval, then?" she asked, confused.

"No. I'm not. I'm not looking for something you can't give."

She nodded and turned back to her work. "Good. Well, I'm glad that's all sorted. Your patient Janie came through her surgery. She's post-op day three and she's doing remarkably well. I think my surgical technique was a complete success. Of course, we'll have to continue to monitor her, but barring any complications I think her prognosis is certainly better than it was."

Sam rolled his eyes as she launched into talking about the procedure and the interviews. As well as all the nitty-gritty medical information that was going to go into the paper she was going to publish in a distinguished medical journal.

He'd never get an apology from his mother because she wasn't wired that way, and he was fine with that now. He hadn't been before and even though he'd prided himself on his mother not influencing him in his career, she had, in a different way.

Now he could move away.

His mother would never change, but at least he understood that now.

Now he had closure.

So he let her talk and just listened.

"Did you get the fellowship you were after?" she finally asked, breaking his chain of thought.

"Yes. I did."

His mother nodded. "Good, but I still think neurosurgery would be a better choice."

"For you, but not for me. I like working with children."

"I never did."

"What?"

"Like working with children. I'm not good with children." A blush tinged her cheek. It was her roundabout way of apologizing to him, without apologizing to him. In her own awkward way she was apologizing for what had happened years ago, for all those nights he'd sat in an OR gallery, reading or playing with his toys by himself, while she'd worked. For eating sandwiches from a vending machine instead of having a home-cooked meal.

When his dad had taken him to Scotland she could've walked away and forgotten about him, but she hadn't. Every summer he'd come to New York and spent time with her, even though he hadn't been with her, but to her, his sitting in the gallery, watching her perform surgery, had been a way for them to connect, and maybe that's why she'd wanted him in neurosurgery as well. As a way to find some common ground, as a way to spend time with him.

And even though it had been a less-than-ideal childhood, spending his summers playing in the hallways of a hospital, at least it had been an attempt.

She hadn't forgotten about him. His mother had just tried the best she could.

Sam grinned. "That's nothing to be ashamed about. We can't all be extraordinary when it comes to pediatrics."

CHAPTER FOURTEEN

MINDY ROLLED HER shoulders. She'd been hunched over her charting for some time. She took off her glasses and set them on her desk, rubbing the bridge of her nose where they'd pinched most, and she tried not to think about Sam.

Of course, that was an exercise in futility, because she couldn't get him out of her mind. Even though the words he'd said had stung, he'd been right.

She was a coward. Instead of facing the supposed rumors, the pitying looks and the laughter, she'd turned tail and run. She could've stayed in Los Angeles and really stuck it to Dean because she was what had made the practice so affluent.

Mindy was tired of running and even though now everyone knew about the dalliance between Sam and her, she wasn't going to leave.

She was here for the long haul.

Of course, she'd heard that he was running away. He was going back to Scotland.

Maybe it's for the best.

Really, what kind of future did they have together? She was older than him, more accomplished, and that might lead to professional jealousy and resentment. Besides Dean being gay, that's also what had happened with their friendship. They'd no longer trusted each other or respected each other.

If he had just come out as gay, that wouldn't have been as bad as the cruel way he'd thrown it in her face. But as she thought back to their relationship, he always had been a bit put out when she'd been given the better surgeries and the attention from their attending.

She'd just been so enamored with the thought of love and marriage that she'd replaced the idea of what love actually was.

But love meant being happy for each other, not trying to bring the other person down.

Love meant being friends. Love meant fighting and making up.

It meant remembering why you were together and sticking it out because, like oxygen, you couldn't live without the other person.

And that's not what she'd had with Dean.

The only person she could think of who fit all those criteria in her head was Sam. Tears stung her eyes, but she wiped them away quickly. She was not going to cry over Sam. He'd made it clear that he didn't want to be with her. He'd go to Scotland and move on.

And so would she. Though it would take some time, she would heal.

There was a knock at the door. She got up, stretching, and opened the door.

"Yes, how can I…?" She trailed off as she looked up to see a six-foot burly Scotsman standing in her doorway. "Dr. Napier, I'm surprised to see you."

"Aye, I can tell by the look on your face. Can I come in?"

Mindy moved to the side and let him into her

office. She shut the door, keeping her back to it just in case she needed to make a quick retreat, and stood there, crossing her arms over her chest. "I thought you were in Scotland?"

"My plane was supposed to leave tonight."

"Supposed? Was it delayed?"

"No. I'm not getting on that plane."

"Well, what are you doing? Attacking me some more? After the way you treated me when I was just making sure you were okay, that was uncalled for."

"Aye, it was."

Mindy was stunned, but then shook her head. No, she wasn't going to fall into his charming trap. She wasn't going to let him off so easily, but that was a harder thing to say than to do. "You hurt me."

"I know."

"I don't think I can forgive you or trust you."

"I understand, but I have something important I need to tell you." Sam took a step toward her. "I'm not going to Scotland. I'm staying at West Manhattan Saints."

"You are?"

"Aye."

"And what, you expect me to leave? I can tell you, you have another thing coming if you think that I'm leaving. I'm not going to turn tail. I'm not a coward."

"No, I know you're not. That was bad form on my part and I don't want you to leave."

"You don't?" she asked, confused.

"No. I've come here to apologize. I was a fool. A pigheaded fool."

"Yes, you were." Mindy relaxed. "So that's all you've come here for? To apologize and tell me you're staying."

"Sort of." His eyes were twinkling. "There was one more thing."

"One more thing?" Her heart began to race and her knees began to shake as he came closer to her, his blue eyes dark and sparkling with tenderness. Just like they'd been when they'd made love. When he'd taken her in his arms and they'd become one.

"Aye," he said, his voice turning husky as he

moved in closer, making her press against the door. "I love you and I aim to earn back your trust. Whatever it takes. I want you, Mindy. Only you."

The words stunned her, to the point she wasn't sure if she'd heard them right. "Sorry, what?"

"I love you. I know I did wrong by you and there is no excuse I can offer you to make that better. I understand if you can't or won't return those feelings, but I wanted you to know that I do love you. I will always love you."

Tears stung Mindy's eyes. She couldn't believe what he was saying. "I thought you didn't want any rumors about dating an attending."

"It doesn't matter now. I know my own worth and let the others talk. I'm not going to be miserable because of what someone else thinks. I love you, Mindy Walker. I will always love you."

Mindy melted. She couldn't deny what she felt and she couldn't stay mad at him any longer. She'd always been afraid of things but she wasn't going to run away from this. "I love you too, but if you ever push me away like that again I'm going to kick you."

"I swear. I never want to hurt you, Mindy. Never again. I can't promise I won't make a *bourach* out of things, but if I do make a mess I promise that I will make it right."

Mindy laughed. "Deal."

Sam grinned. "Good. I'm glad. I think I'm going to kiss you now—that okay?"

"Aye," she said, tears rolling down her cheeks.

Sam laughed and then pulled her into his arms and kissed her, like it was the first time all over again. Like the slate had been wiped clean and there was nothing between them now. The ghosts of their pasts were wiped clean; it was just the two of them.

Two fools in love.

His hands were wrapped around her, holding her close and making her feel safe. This was what love was and Mindy didn't want to let it go. She was never going to let this go.

When the kiss ended she smiled up at him. "Just one condition."

Sam cocked an eyebrow. "There are conditions now?"

"Just one. I'm not traveling to Brooklyn to stay in an apartment in a house full of residents and fellows."

"What're you suggesting, then?"

"That you take all those boxes you packed and move into a certain penthouse apartment down the street."

Sam laughed. "Well, my roommates might not be happy about me vacating but, aye, I'll agree to your term as long as you agree to mine."

"You think you're in a position to bargain?"

"Aye."

"So what is your term?"

"That you shut up and kiss me again."

"I can agree to that term." And she fulfilled her end of the bargain promptly.

EPILOGUE

Three months later

MINDY WALKED ALONG the halls of West Manhattan Saints toward the NICU. She was grinning ear to ear. It was spring and she loved days like this. Mostly she was glad the cold, sucktacular winter was over.

As she walked down the hall Sam came up beside her, and he was grinning as well.

"You're very happy today," Mindy teased.

"So are you!"

"It's spring." She took a sip of her coffee. "I love spring."

"Come on, you survived your first New York winter. You should be proud of that."

"I am proud of that! Who said I wasn't?"

"No one." Sam chuckled. "Are you ready for the big day?"

"Of course I'm ready for this day. This day is another reason why today is my favorite day. It's spring and the quints are going home."

Sam chuckled. "Yeah, today is a good day."

He reached down and grabbed her hand, squeezing it, making her blush. She was so happy with Sam. They'd been together three months, but it felt like longer than that. His roommates had grumbled about him leaving, but it had only been half-hearted. They'd been happy for him.

It had been a huge step, asking him to move in with her. She usually didn't move so fast with relationships, but then again this was different from her relationship with Dean. It was right to move it along so fast.

There was surprisingly no animosity at the hospital, because Chief Langley made sure that everyone knew she had nothing to do with Sam getting one of the pediatric fellowship spots and Mindy was able to be open about her relationship with Sam.

They weren't trying to hide anything.

She was positive there were still rumors floating around about them, but frankly she didn't care anymore. There were always going to be gossips.

Even Sam had come to terms with the fact that everyone knew his mother was Dr. Monica Hanley. Some doctors still referred to him as Dr. Hanley's son, which vexed him no end, but you couldn't change people and Mindy learned you can't live your life worrying about what other people thought of you, because that was no life worth living at all.

Mindy had let go of her anger toward Dean and Owen, and in her heart she forgave them. Sam had taught her to trust again and that was worth moving on for.

Once their busy period was over and they both had some vacation time, Sam promised to take her to Scotland to meet his father and the rest of his family. Although he warned her that his gran wouldn't be pleased that she'd ruined the sweater she'd knitted for him.

"Gran is a teetotaler. She won't be happy

you ruined the sweater by spilling Scotch all over me."

"Are you going to tell her you were the one drinking said Scotch?"

"No. I'm not a fool."

Sam brought her out of her reverie. "I love you." He bent down and kissed her on the lips in the middle of the busy hall of the hospital.

"Dr. Napier, I can't go into that press conference with you holding my hand and kissing me like that."

"Of course you can." He pulled her to a side hallway. "Have you reconsidered my question?"

Mindy shook her head. "I'm not answering that question right now."

"Oh, aye?"

"Aye. I have to concentrate on this press conference. I'm not used to press conferences."

"You'll be fine."

"We should call your mother in from Harvard to do this. After all, she did take care of Michael Jameson's shunt."

Sam groaned. "It took three months to get

her to go back to Harvard. Haven't I suffered enough?"

"No." Mindy kissed him on the cheek.

"Thanks."

"At least you have to go up there and talk about Michael. Since you were his primary pediatrician."

"Dr. Chang is, I'm just a fellow."

"Dr. Chang is on vacation and as her fellow you have to fill in for her."

"You're enjoying this, aren't you?" Sam asked.

"I am." Mindy grinned and then swiped her card to open the NICU. "Come on, then."

Sam followed her into the NICU, into a private room where Mr. and Mrs. Jameson were waiting with five very special bundles of joy.

"Dr. Napier, Dr. Walker!" Mrs. Jameson exclaimed.

"Good morning," Mindy said. "Have they photographed the babies yet?"

Mrs. Jameson nodded. "They have. Does that mean we can go?"

"Yes, you can go," Sam said. "All the babies

are healthy; they've all passed their car-seat tests with flying colors. You can take them home."

"So you don't need them for that press conference that's gathered downstairs?" Mr. Jameson asked.

"No. You're not needed for that," Mindy said. "Take your babies home. It's been a long time coming."

Mrs. Jameson's eyes filled with tears. "Thank you both. And give my thanks to Dr. Hanley and Dr. Chang as well. Actually...I think there are too many people to thank."

"We know. You don't need to thank us. It was our pleasure." Mindy gave Mrs. Jameson a hug.

"Keep us posted with pictures."

"I will." Mrs. Jameson was beaming as she and Mr. Jameson loaded five car-seat carriers into a large stroller that had been specially fashioned for them.

Mindy and Sam left the NICU and headed toward the conference room. As they got closer they could hear the buzz of a crowd. Journalists were waiting to hear about West Manhattan

Saints' first quintuplet delivery and she knew they were also waiting to see the quints. Too bad they would be disappointed.

She was about to open the door, but Sam stopped her.

"No, this isn't happening."

Mindy was shocked as he grabbed her by the arm and frog-marched her once again into a private room, shutting the door behind him.

"What are you doing?"

"I'm not letting you out of this room until you answer the question I asked you this morning."

"Sam, aren't we rushing things?"

He cocked an eyebrow. "How are we rushing things? Three months ago I moved in with you and now you're telling me that soon I'm going to be a father, so me asking you to marry me is rushing things?"

Mindy sighed. "I was married once before."

"I swear I won't cheat on you with your best friend."

"You're my best friend."

"Aye, well, if you become my wife then I won't have to cheat on you with myself."

Mindy laughed. "That makes no sense."

"Well, you not giving me an answer to my proposal makes no sense either."

She smiled. "Why don't we have the baby first and then talk marriage."

He shook his head. "That's backwards. We have to do this the traditional way."

"What has been traditional about this?"

"Nothing, but I aim to rectify that." He took a step toward her and cupped her face in his hands. "I love you, Mindy. That's never going to change."

Her heart skipped a beat. "I love you too."

"So?"

Tears filled her eyes and this time she couldn't stop them. Usually she was quite good at it, but she was blaming it on the pregnancy hormones. "Yes. I'll marry you."

Sam pulled her into his arms and kissed her, making her knees go weak. When he pulled away she moaned in protest.

"You have a press conference, remember?"

"Do we have to go?" she whined.

"You're the one who said we did." Sam kissed her again. "Come on. You can do this. I have a feeling with the reputation you're getting here at West Manhattan Saints that this won't be the last. I think it's the first of many."

Mindy took his hand. "I'm ready."

And she was. She was ready to face just about anything, as long as she had Sam.

* * * * *

Don't miss the other stories in the fabulous
NEW YORK CITY DOCS *series*
Available now!

MILLS & BOON®
Large Print Medical

April

The Baby of Their Dreams	Carol Marinelli
Falling for Her Reluctant Sheikh	Amalie Berlin
Hot-Shot Doc, Secret Dad	Lynne Marshall
Father for Her Newborn Baby	Lynne Marshall
His Little Christmas Miracle	Emily Forbes
Safe in the Surgeon's Arms	Molly Evans

May

A Touch of Christmas Magic	Scarlet Wilson
Her Christmas Baby Bump	Robin Gianna
Winter Wedding in Vegas	Janice Lynn
One Night Before Christmas	Susan Carlisle
A December to Remember	Sue MacKay
A Father This Christmas?	Louisa Heaton

June

Playboy Doc's Mistletoe Kiss	Tina Beckett
Her Doctor's Christmas Proposal	Louisa George
From Christmas to Forever?	Marion Lennox
A Mummy to Make Christmas	Susanne Hampton
Miracle Under the Mistletoe	Jennifer Taylor
His Christmas Bride-to-Be	Abigail Gordon

MILLS & BOON®
Large Print Medical

July

A Daddy for Baby Zoe?	Fiona Lowe
A Love Against All Odds	Emily Forbes
Her Playboy's Proposal	Kate Hardy
One Night...with Her Boss	Annie O'Neil
A Mother for His Adopted Son	Lynne Marshall
A Kiss to Change Her Life	Karin Baine

August

His Shock Valentine's Proposal	Amy Ruttan
Craving Her Ex-Army Doc	Amy Ruttan
The Man She Could Never Forget	Meredith Webber
The Nurse Who Stole His Heart	Alison Roberts
Her Holiday Miracle	Joanna Neil
Discovering Dr Riley	Annie Claydon

September

The Socialite's Secret	Carol Marinelli
London's Most Eligible Doctor	Annie O'Neil
Saving Maddie's Baby	Marion Lennox
A Sheikh to Capture Her Heart	Meredith Webber
Breaking All Their Rules	Sue MacKay
One Life-Changing Night	Louisa Heaton